Christmas with Mr Darcy

Victoria Connelly

Cuthland Press

Copyright © 2012 Victoria Connelly

www.victoriaconnelly.com

Victoria Connelly asserts the moral right to be identified as the
author of this work.

Cover image by Roy Connelly

Published by Cuthland Press

This paperback edition first published 2013

Ebook edition first published 2012

ISBN-13: 978-0-9569866-6-5

To Toni and Joe. We miss you guys!

ACKNOWLEDGMENTS

First of all, I'd like to thank to all my lovely readers who have enjoyed the Austen Addicts Trilogy. Your kind messages are much cherished and I sincerely hope you like this little sequel.

Special thanks to two wonderful friends who have shared their passion and knowledge of Jane Austen with me: Jane Odiwe and Amanda Grange. I adore your books!

And heartfelt thanks to three very special ladies who have shone a spotlight on my trilogy: Laurel Ann Nattress, Maria Grazia and Meredith Esparza. Your support is much appreciated. Also, a big thank you to Ann Channon at The Jane Austen House Museum in Chawton for giving me the very great pleasure of seeing a copy of one of my books in Jane Austen's home.

Thanks to Jo Nadin, Rowan Coleman and Heather Zerfahs, Nicki Mattey, Dana Hartl Cally Taylor, Katrina Ray, Evelyn Krenkel, Jennifer Gardner Poellinger, Alexandra Brown, Viv Hampshire, Gail Mallin, Joanna Jacobs and Tina Campion for super-fast work getting me out of a potential pickle!

And, as ever, to my husband Roy.

* * *

'One cannot have too large a party. A large party secures its own amusement.' – Jane Austen, *Emma*

* * *

CHAPTER 1

There were few sights more beautiful in Hampshire than Purley Hall in the snow. The faded red-bricked Georgian manor house stood proudly in the middle of the white landscape as if it were at the centre of a snow globe, and the fields surrounding it were smooth and sparkling in the December sunlight.

The little village of Church Stinton looked like a Christmas card. Thatched roofs had been dusted with sugar-like snow, and the church was postcard-pretty, its great yew trees looking ethereal under their white cloaks.

The south of England had been surprised by the first snow of the year but it hadn't been hit as badly as the north of the country and, after a week of commuter chaos, the snow was beginning to disappear. Still, as Dame Pamela Harcourt looked out of the hall window, she couldn't help feeling anxious.

'Can you believe that more snow has been forecast? You don't think it will put people off coming do you?' she asked her brother. She'd been hosting Jane Austen conferences for several years now and not one had been cancelled yet.

'Pammy, earthquakes and tornadoes couldn't keep Austen fans away,' Dan said from his position at the top of a ladder as he threaded a long garland of golden stars around the Christmas tree.

Dame Pamela's twitchy fingers reached up to the pearl choker she was wearing. It was ten o'clock in the morning but, with her billowing red velvet tunic and pearls adorning her ears, throat and wrists, she looked more suitable for a red-carpet event than a morning at home.

She moved to stand under the enormous Christmas tree which had taken four men to place in the entrance hall. It was to be decorated in red, green and gold, and it was going to look perfect with its twinkling lights and heap of shiny, beribboned presents stacked underneath.

'Pass me the baubles,' Dan said a moment later and Dame Pamela handed him the first of the glass baubles. They gleamed like fat rubies in the light of the hall and she watched as they were placed oh-so-carefully at intervals around the tree.

'You really are very good at this,' she told her brother.

'I should be after the number of times I've done it,' he said, turning around and smiling at her.

'My wonderful little brother!' she said. 'What would I do without you?' She looked at his handsome profile and his shock of red-gold hair. She adored him and had been absolutely delighted when he'd married young Robyn – one of the attendees of a past Jane Austen conference. And now they had a little daughter, Cassandra. She smiled. She had a lot to thank Jane Austen for. Not only had the she provided her with an adorable sister-in-law but she had done wonders for her career too because Dame Pamela had had the privilege of playing Elizabeth Bennet and Marianne Dashwood in TV adaptations of Austen's novels in her youth, and Lady Catherine de Bourgh and Fanny Ferrars Dashwood in more recent years. And then there were the conferences which she so looked forward to. It had started off with an annual conference in the autumn but that had proved so popular that she had decided to host a special Christmas conference too and no expense was going to be spared.

Every guest bedroom had been decorated with evergreen garlands over the fireplaces and picture frames. A new dinner service had been bought: white edged with gold. There were crystal wine glasses too and enormous flower displays threaded with fairy lights. Great green garlands adorned the enormous front door and lights had been placed in the trees lining the driveway. Dame Pamela had also insisted that the temple on the island should be decorated with lights.

Purley Hall had to look its very best for Christmas. Even if Dame Pamela was away from home at that time of year, decorations were still insisted upon but this year was even more special than usual because it was the very first Jane Austen Christmas conference. She smiled as she thought about the programme that lay ahead. There would be parlour games and competitions, there would be special guests and dancing – *lots* of dancing! It was going to be glorious – the very best Jane Austen conference yet. She said that every year, of course, but this time she really meant it.

They had even found 'The Purley Angel' for the top of the Christmas tree. It had gone missing for years in one of the attic rooms but had been unearthed by Higgins the butler in a valiant expedition. He'd emerged from the attic, his grey hair even greyer than usual with cobwebs, and his bright blue waistcoat dulled with dust.

Dame Pamela looked up at the old-fashioned angel now. The pale face was a little scuffed and Higgins had had to sew up a tiny tear in her gold dress but her gossamer wings were perfect and looked as if they were about to lift her to the very heavens.

'There,' Dan said a moment later as he came back down to earth from the ladder. The two of them stood side by side admiring their work. The tree looked wonderful – like something that would grace a magazine cover.

'Do you think it's *enough*?' Dame Pamela asked. 'I mean, one can never have too many baubles.'

Dan shook his head. 'No more baubles, Pammy. The tree will topple right over if we overload it and we don't want any squashed Janeites, do we?'

'Perish the thought!' she said.

It was then that Higgins the butler appeared, his gold waistcoat looking very Christmassy indeed.

'What is it, Higgins?' Dame Pamela asked.

'Master Benedict has just been on the telephone,' Higgins announced. 'He said he'll be arriving in time for lunch.'

Dame Pamela frowned. '*Benedict?*'

'Indeed,' Higgins said.

'But I didn't invite him,' Dame Pamela said. 'Did you?' She turned to her brother.

Dan shook his head. 'Certainly not! It seems like he's invited himself.'

Dame Pamela took in a very deep breath and then sighed it back out. 'Oh, dear!' she said. 'That's *all* we need!'

CHAPTER 2

Robyn Love Harcourt was writing the last of her Christmas cards. She'd left it horribly late this year but she'd been so busy organising the Christmas conference with Dame Pamela that her own private little Christmas had been put on hold. Still, it had all been such enormous fun. She'd been working happily as Dame Pamela's PA since accepting the job offer after her first weekend at Purley and had fallen into her new role as if she'd been performing it her whole life.

Together, they had pored over hundreds of magazines and websites for inspiration for the Christmas conference and, Robyn couldn't help thinking with a laugh, perhaps they'd spent a little too much time discussing colour schemes.

'Is pink and purple a bit too much?' Dame Pamela had asked at one point, having found a company that sold pink glitter-ball baubles.

Robyn had been swept along by the idea of Purley Hall decked out in romantic shades of pink and lustrous shades of purple but had then come back down to earth.

'I think we'd better keep things traditional,' she'd said at last, secretly craving the pink baubles they'd discovered. Perhaps Dan would let her decorate their own tree with them. She could just imagine how pretty Horseshoe Cottage would look. She'd already secretly purchased a couple of gingerbread garlands and two ropes of multi-coloured fairy lights which baby Cassie had loved when Robyn had switched them on.

Once again, Robyn felt the warm glow of pride when she thought about her little girl. She still couldn't believe how her life had changed since coming to the Jane Austen conference. She'd fallen madly in love with her host's younger brother, Dan Harcourt, and she couldn't believe that he'd returned her feelings. It had all been such a whirlwind. She'd given up her job in North Yorkshire and had driven herself and her hens all the way down to Hampshire to start her new life. She smiled as she remembered that dreadful journey with Lizzie, Lydia, Mrs Bennet, Lady Catherine, Miss Bingley and Wickham the cockerel. Named after characters from *Pride and Prejudice*, Robyn had since added three ex-factory hens to her flock: Elinor, Marianne and Emma. They'd arrived at Horseshoe Cottage with pale combs and threadbare breasts but they had embraced their new free-range life and had bloomed into beautiful birds.

Robyn would often laugh with Dan at the life they'd created for themselves. There were dogs, horses, hens and a baby. It was permanent chaos but she wouldn't have it any other way.

Finishing the last of her Christmas cards and determining to get them in the post that day, Robyn wrapped Cassie up in her pink winter shawl, pushed a scarlet woolly hat onto her head and then plopped her into her buggy. It was an amazing buggy – Cassie's own little four-wheel drive - which allowed them to face the very fiercest of footpaths and took the potholed lane to Horseshoe Cottage in its stride. Robyn pulled on her winter coat – a practical knee-length waxed jacket which Dame Pamela had bought her shortly after she'd moved to Hampshire.

'You have to have wax if you're going to live in the country,' she'd told her and Robyn was now a convert. She loved the big deep pockets which could house all manner of things including a week's supply of dog biscuits.

Shoving her feet inside a pair of sturdy walking boots and squashing one of Dan's tweed caps down onto her curls, Robyn and Cassie set out for Purley Hall, shutting the front door quickly before Biscuit and Moby could dash out into the lane, promising them a good walk later. She'd been given the morning off as they'd been working late the night before but she couldn't wait any longer to see the Christmas tree.

'Let's surprise Daddy and Aunt Pammy,' she said to Cassie.

The lane looked magical under its light covering of snow although it made negotiating the potholes all the more difficult. Robyn took her time, pointing out the bright holly berries that lined the hedge and laughing when a robin landed right beside them.

The air was crisp and Robyn's breath turned into a little cloud in front of her face and her fingers were quickly numbed. She reached inside her voluminous pockets for her woolly gloves, glad of their warm comfort despite the fact that they smelled of Bonio.

Taking the road into the village, she turned right along the driveway to Purley Hall. It was a route that she would never tire of for each season leant it its own beauty and it was particularly stunning in the snow with the bare branches of the trees rimed in white.

Cassie's buggy made it comfortably up the driveway, leaving a set of neat tracks behind it. Reaching the steps before the front door, Robyn used the boot scraper to remove the worst of the snow and then unclipped Cassie and scooped her up.

'Look at the garland, Cassie!' she said, pointing above the door where an evergreen garland was threaded with bright holly berries and large golden bows.

There was no need to knock on the door because it was unlocked and Robyn stepped inside, feeling the warmth instantly embracing her. It was then that she saw the funniest sight – her husband was balancing precariously on top of a step ladder with his hand up an angel's dress.

'Dan!' she cried.

Dan turned around, toppled dangerously for a moment and then got down from the ladder.

'Robyn!' he said in surprise. 'What are you doing here?'

'I've come to see my favourite husband, of course!'

'Liar!' he said. 'You've come to see the tree.'

'Well, that too,' she said with a smile. 'It looks wonderful!' The lights had been turned on and were twinkling amongst the dark branches and the gold, red and green baubles shone brightly.

'It does, doesn't it?' Dan said, 'only I can't seem to get this angel straight.'

Robyn cocked her head to one side. 'She does look as if she's had one glass of mulled wine too many.'

Dan nodded. 'But at least this little angel looks perfect!' he said, bending down to kiss his daughter's pink cheek before kissing Robyn fully on the mouth. 'Had a good morning?'

'We have. I've finished all the Christmas cards at last. They're going to be horribly late but that can't be helped.'

'Don't worry about it,' he said, removing the tweed cap from her head and running his fingers through her blonde curls. 'You've been so tied up with all this conference stuff, I'm sure people will understand.'

'I hope so. I feel awful about it.'

'You worry too much,' Dan said. 'You've got to relax more.'

Robyn nodded. 'I guess,' she said. 'Where's Pammy? I thought she'd be decorating the tree with you.'

'Ah!' Dan said.

'What?'

'She's trying to avoid a catastrophe.'

'What do you mean?'

'It seems we'll be having an extra guest for Christmas.'

'Really? Who?'

'Benedict.'

'Your brother?'

'One of them,' Dan said. He actually had more brothers than he could keep track of but none of them really kept in touch – they were all so busy leading their own lives with their own families. 'I can't help thinking it would be so much easier if it was any one of them other than Benedict.'

Robyn frowned. 'You've never really told me much about your brothers,' she said.

'And with good reason.'

'So tell me now,' she said.

Dan sighed. 'Benedict is trouble,' he said. 'He's always in some fix or other and expects Pammy to rescue him.'

'And does she?'

'Well, she has in the past but it's cost her dearly and he never seems to learn his lesson.'

'What does he do – gamble?'

'Not gambling as such – he's more into risky business ventures that he's convinced will make him a millionaire only they tend to go wrong and he ends up in debt.'

'Oh, dear.' For a moment, Robyn remembered one of Jane Austen's brothers, Henry, who had become bankrupt.

'So, he's probably the last person Pammy wants turning up just as she's hosting a Jane Austen conference,' Dan said.

Just then, Dame Pamela entered the hallway. 'Robyn!' she cried. 'I thought you were having the morning off.'

'I am. I just couldn't resist taking a peek at the tree.'

'Isn't it splendid?' Dame Pamela enthused.

'Yes,' Robyn said. 'I'm so glad we went for traditional colours in the end.'

'Me too,' Dame Pamela said, 'although perhaps we could try pink and purple next Christmas.'

Dan rolled his eyes at the pair of them.

'And how is my adorable niece?' Dame Pamela asked, taking Cassie from Robyn and kissing her forehead.

'Did you speak to Benedict?' Dan asked.

'I can't get hold of him,' Dame Pamela said. 'He's not answering his mobile.'

'Of course he isn't,' Dan said, 'because he knows you'd try to stop him coming here.'

'What are we going to do?'

'I don't think there's a lot we can do,' Dan said.

'But he can't stay here,' Dame Pamela said. 'I mean we've got room but it just wouldn't work with the conference on. He's bound to cause trouble of some sort – he always does!'

'He can stay at ours if you prefer,' Dan said.

'Oh, darling! There isn't room at your little cottage and I wouldn't dare inflict him on poor Robyn!'

'I'm looking forward to meeting him,' Robyn said.

Dame Pamela looked at her in alarm. 'My dear girl – Benedict Harcourt isn't someone you look forward to meeting. He's somebody you look forward to leaving.'

Robyn grinned. 'Where does he live?'

'York is the last I heard,' Dame Pamela said.

'Well, Yorkshire has five inches of snow already,' Robyn pointed out, thinking of the county she used to call home. 'Maybe he won't be able to get here.'

'Oh, he'll get here all right. He's probably going to try and spend the whole of the Christmas holidays here,' Dame Pamela said with a sigh.

'And New Year,' Dan said. 'He knows that New Year at Purley is too good to miss.'

'Yes, the last one he spent here, he got through nine bottles of vintage champagne,' Dame Pamela said. 'Now, I really must talk to Higgins about this and see if there's something we can do.'

'Yes, like locking away all the silver!' Dan said.

'Don't even joke about it!' Dame Pamela said, leaving the room in hasty chase of her trusty butler.

'Goodness!' Robyn said. 'I hope everything's going to be okay. As if this threat of snow isn't bad enough.' She walked over to the window and peered up at the sepia-coloured sky.

'Listen - you're living in the south now, remember?' Dan said. 'The snow is much more civilized here.'

'But we've had two cancellations already,' Robyn pointed out.

'Lightweights!' he said. 'Call themselves Austen fans?'

12

'I'm really worried. I hope it isn't going to be a washout.'

'It won't be,' Dan said, placing his hands on her shoulders. 'It's going to be brilliant. It always is, isn't it?'

Robyn nodded. The Jane Austen conferences at Purley Hall were building in popularity and all the bed and breakfasts in the vicinity would be booked up months in advance and, the summer before, Dame Pamela had decided to convert the part of the stable block that Dan used to live in. Now, there were three beautiful ensuite bedrooms for guests who didn't mind the smell of horses.

Robyn had been in two minds about the conversion. On the one hand, she was delighted that the conferences were gaining more interest and she loved the role she played in organising everything alongside her new boss but she couldn't help missing the little flat where her husband had once lived. It was a special part of their history and she felt sad that she could no longer walk up those wooden stairs and stand in the rooms where they'd shared so many special moments.

But she knew that they were so lucky to have Horseshoe Cottage and she thanked her lucky stars every day for the good fortune that had brought her to Hampshire and to Dan.

'We'd better get organised, then,' Robyn said as she looked at the Queen Anne clock above the mantelpiece. 'The first guests will be arriving soon.'

Dan nodded. 'And I've *got* to do something about that drunken angel.'

CHAPTER 3

After entrusting her two beloved cats, Freddie and Fitz, to her neighbour for the Christmas holidays, Katherine Roberts had left her Oxfordshire cottage and had joined Warwick Lawton at his home in West Sussex. She loved staying at the Georgian manor house with its huge sash windows and views out across the South Downs. The Old Vicarage was an imposing house and perfect for a writer of Regency romance with its lofty ceilings and pleasing Georgian symmetry. It reminded Katherine of Purley Hall – the home of Dame Pamela Harcourt - only The Old Vicarage was a far more modest property and perfectly suited to the life of a bachelor who didn't really have time to worry about a bigger property.

Katherine never tired of browsing through the miles and miles of bookshelves that seemed to line every wall in the house. The rooms were light and elegant and perfect for reading in but she couldn't help redecorating a few of them in her mind. As she sat in the rather shabby armchairs that seemed to be placed by each of the windows of the house, she would often lower the book she was reading and gaze around her.

Those curtains need replacing, she would think. *That sofa needs re-upholstering and this rug has seen better days.*

Then she would check herself. *This is not your house*, she would say.

Although Katherine never liked to miss one of Purley Hall's conferences, she couldn't help wishing that they were just going to have a quiet Christmas together at Warwick's. They both led such busy lives and it wasn't always easy to find time just to relax together. Katherine had a punishing timetable at St Bridget's College in Oxford and, by the time one of them had travelled to stay with the other, the weekend seemed as if it was already over.

Katherine sighed. Something was going to have to change at some point, she could see that, but what? They hadn't talked much about their future together; they'd been happy enough to go from day to day but how long would that last? Would they want to live together and who would be the one to compromise?

Warwick adored The Old Vicarage and Katherine couldn't bear the thought of asking him to give it up and how would she feel if he refused? Equally, she hated the thought of leaving her little cottage in the Oxfordshire countryside. It was everything a cottage should be with its beams and sloping floors and bulging walls on which paintings would never hang straight but its tiny proportions weren't made for two. Whenever Warwick stayed, he was always banging his head on the low beams and doorframes. Plus there was the fact that her job was in Oxford and she couldn't give that up. She'd worked so hard for her place in academia and she couldn't imagine leaving it.

But she wasn't going to worry herself about that now. They had the Christmas conference to look forward to. They were travelling together in Warwick's Jaguar but it was a journey that worried Katherine.

'Are you sure it'll make it if it snows?' she asked as she got into the car, winding a plum-coloured around her neck.

'It isn't going to snow,' Warwick told her.

Katherine looked out of the window and up into the slate-coloured sky. 'Are you *sure*?'

'Look, you might hold the doctorate in this relationship but I know about weather and – trust me – it isn't going to snow,' Warwick said.

Forty minutes later, the first fine flakes of snow had started to fall from the heavens and Katherine glared at Warwick from the passenger seat.

'We'll be there in no time, don't you worry,' he said, picking up speed.

Katherine was looking forward to visiting Purley Hall again although she wanted to be sure she got there in one piece. They'd revisited since they'd met at the Jane Austen conference because one of Warwick's novels had been adapted into a film for television and part of it had been shot at Purley, and Katherine had given a talk at the October conference just two months ago.

'Adam Craig's going to be there, isn't he?' Katherine said, remembering the affable producer who had worked on the film.

'He's giving a talk about his adaptation of *Persuasion*.'

'Wonderful!' Katherine said. 'I did love it. I thought Gemma Reilly was just perfect as Anne Elliot.'

'Apparently, Gemma's going to be there too!' Warwick said.

'Really? Did Dame Pamela tell you that?'

Warwick nodded with a little smile. There hadn't been an official programme sent out ahead of the special Christmas conference but, since Warwick's novel had been filmed at Purley, he'd had a direct line to the owner and was privy to all sorts of information.

'I can't wait to see everyone again,' Katherine said, knowing she could catch up with Robyn and Dan and see little Cassie, and she hoped that dear old Doris Norris would be there too. 'Oh, God!' she suddenly said.

'What?'

'You don't think Mrs Soames will be there, do you?' she asked.

'To spoil everyone's Christmas, you mean? Of *course* she'll be there. She wouldn't miss such a ripe opportunity as that,' Warwick said with a laugh.

'I hope you're wrong!' Katherine said, thinking of the run-ins she'd had with the odious woman in the past.

'It'll be funny actually staying there together again, won't it? I mean, the last time,' he paused, 'well, it was the first time – for us.'

Katherine felt herself blushing because she was remembering it too. 'Yes, I met a real idiot there who ran his suitcase over my foot and spun some silly story about being an antiquarian.'

'Hey! *You're* the one who started that antiquarian business, not *me!*' Warwick said.

'Oh, and you were so quick to correct me, weren't you, *Lorna?*' Katherine said, giving him the tiniest of smiles.

'You're not still mad, are you?' Warwick asked. When he'd first met Katherine, he hadn't told her the complete truth about who he really was and it had got him into a lot of trouble.

'No, of course I'm not mad,' she said.

'Good because that would make this weekend very difficult.'

'Why?' she asked.

'Just because,' he said.

'Are you planning something?'

'I couldn't possibly say,' he said, grinning to himself as he turned onto the main road and hit the accelerator.

In a neat red-bricked Victorian house in a quiet backstreet of Winchester, just a stone's throw away from Jane Austen's resting place in the cathedral, Mia Castle was beside herself with worry.

'I think I should take him with me,' she told her sister, 'or maybe not go at all.'

'Don't be silly, Mia!' Sarah told her. 'Gabe is perfectly capable of looking after William on his own.'

'I know he is.'

'And you wouldn't want to miss the chance to chat to Dame Pamela Harcourt, would you?'

Mia grinned. 'I can't believe I'm going to stay at her house!' For a moment, Mia thought about the time she'd attended an event with Dame Pamela at the Jane Austen Festival in Bath and how her friend, Shelley, had dared to tell the great actress that Mia wanted to be an actress too. Since leaving drama school, Mia still harboured those dreams deep inside herself but life had been a little more complicated than she'd anticipated and she'd found herself a single mother to young William and had had to put her dreams on hold.

'And you left Will to go to the Jane Austen Festival in Bath, didn't you?' Sarah reminded her.

'Yes but that wasn't for so long,' Mia said, tying her long dark hair back into a pony tail.

'You'll be back with him in no time at all,' Sarah said, 'besides, you can't go all the way to Bath now to pick up Will because we'd be late for the conference and you know how much I hate being late.'

Mia knew only too well. Her sister, Sarah, suffered from OCD – Obsessive Compulsive Disorder - which gave her innumerable quirks such as not being able to watch a programme on television if the credits had already started rolling before she'd sat down; she had to be there at the very beginning of things otherwise it would be spoilt and she wouldn't be able to settle.

The Christmas conference would be the first they'd attended at Purley Hall and they were both looking forward to it. They'd just been reunited at the Jane Austen Festival in Bath after three years apart from each other. Mia was living there now with her architect partner, Gabe, and her two-year old son, William. His full name was William Fitz – in honour of Fitzwilliam Darcy. When she'd found out she was having a boy, she'd debated calling him Fitzwilliam but had decided that it would probably be a cruel thing to do to a modern child.

'Anyway, I think Gabe's going to really appreciate some time alone with William. You've seen how well they've bonded. They're going to love their time together,' Sarah said.

'You make it sound like I won't be missed at all!' Mia said with a pout.

'You know what I mean!' Sarah said, ruffling her younger sister's hair.

'It's a shame Lloyd isn't coming with us,' Mia said, thinking of her brother-in-law to be.

7

'I know. He really wanted to but that job up in Scotland was too good to miss,' Sarah said.

'I adored his photos of the Jane Austen Festival in *Vive!*,' Mia said.

'Yes,' Sarah said. 'He seems to tolerate my Austen addiction really well.'

'You surely wouldn't be thinking of marrying a man who *didn't* like Jane Austen, would you?' Mia teased.

Sarah shook her head. She'd been married once before and it had caused a split between her and her sister. A split she never wanted to experience again because she loved her sister more than life itself.

'Lloyd understands you so well,' Mia continued.

'I'm lucky to have found him,' Sarah said as she straightened a tablecloth that really didn't need straightening. 'Now, help me tidy this place up before we leave.'

'Tidy what? It's immaculate already!' Mia said, knowing that her sister wouldn't be happy until everything had been vacuumed yet again and every cushion and curtain had been plumped and straightened.

'We're not going until it's absolutely right,' Sarah said.

Mia smiled at her sister, knowing that her Jane Austen weekend wasn't going to start until *everything* was perfect.

Kay Ashton looked out of her bedroom window at Wentworth House in Lyme Regis and gazed out at the grey sea. She loved the Dorset coast in winter. It had a bleak beauty about it that might not appeal to everybody but Kay adored it.

Winter was a quiet time for Kay. The holiday-makers had long gone and running the bed and breakfast took a back seat which meant that Kay could dedicate herself to her true passion: painting.

Kay had always painted. She loved the freedom that a brush allowed and, after putting together a series of Austen-inspired paintings for two books called *The*

Illustrated Darcy and *The Illustrated Wentworth* which was going to be published by a small London publisher, Kay had turned to her beloved Dorset and was concentrating on landscapes. But she didn't have time for any painting now. She had to pack because Adam would be arriving at any moment. He'd persuaded her to shut the bed and breakfast over the Christmas period. It was usually a quiet time anyway and he'd told Kay that she needed a break – a good break.

Turning around to face the clothes she'd laid out on the bed, she smiled as she remembered him telling her about Purley Hall. Adam was a screenwriter and film producer and he'd recently filmed an adaptation of a Lorna Warwick novel at the Georgian manor house in Hampshire and had fallen in love with the place and was desperate to share it with her.

'You'll love it!' he'd enthused. But what Kay loved more was the idea of a Jane Austen conference. She'd never heard of anything like it before. A conference dedicated to Jane Austen – how marvellous was that?

She was just reaching for her sketchpad when she heard the door opening downstairs.

'Kay?'

'I'm upstairs, Adam.'

She heard him take the stairs two at a time and he was in the room before she could draw breath, taking her in his arms and kissing her.

'How are you?' he said at last.

'Thoroughly kissed!' she said with a little laugh.

'I always like to start as I mean to go on,' he said. He was wearing a thick wool jumper in chocolate brown that only had a couple of ginger cat hairs on it.

'Did you take Sir Walter round to Nana's?' she asked, running her fingers through his short dark hair.

'Yes,' Adam said, 'although he was a devil to get into the basket. I think he knew what was coming.'

'Oh, he'll be spoilt rotten there,' Kay said. 'Your nana always gives him the best of everything.'

'I know,' he said. 'I only wish she could come with us.'

'Nana Craig would *not* like that!' Kay said.

'Why not?' he asked, pushing his glasses up his nose.

'Because there will be actors there, of course!'

'Ah, yes!' Adam said with a little laugh. His dear old nana had detested actors ever since her husband had run off with an actress several decades ago. She'd never trusted them and had been mightily relieved when Adam had become involved with Kay and not that Gemma Reilly actress woman who had been hanging around Lyme Regis during the filming of the recent adaptation of *Persuasion*.

'It will be so lovely to see Gemma again,' Kay said.

Adam nodded. 'Just as long as you're not going to try and match-make me and her again!'

'Oh, Adam!' Kay said with a smile. 'That was nothing more than a little mistake.' She encircled her arms around his waist and kissed him. 'I should have known that there was no other woman for you but *me*.'

CHAPTER 4

Later that afternoon, the entrance hall of Purley was filled with excited chatter as the guests arrived and everybody stood in line to be allocated their rooms. Old friends greeted each other with screams of joy and warm embraces, and Robyn and Dan handed out keys and pointed people in the right direction.

'Oh, just look at that tree!' Doris Norris said, her pale eyes shining brightly as she gazed up into its branches. 'But isn't that angel a bit-' she paused and cocked her head to one side.

'What?' Robyn asked her.

'Skewiff?'

Robyn sighed and caught Dan's eye.

'What?' he asked.

'The angel's drunk again,' she said

Doris Norris giggled. 'She's not the only one,' she said. 'I had a little glass of sherry before I came out to warm me up and I think it's gone right to my head!'

Robyn linked arms with her. 'Then we'll get you straight to your room so you can have a nice rest before the welcome reception.'

'Excuse me!' a voice suddenly boomed from behind Robyn and she turned to come face to face with her old adversary.

'Can I help you, Mrs Soames?'

'Well, I'm not sure that you can. You seem *much* too young to be in charge of anything important,' Mrs Soames declared, her face red and her bosom pushed up high in front of her.

Robyn tried not to bristle at the comment. 'If you don't tell me what's wrong, I won't be of any help at all, will I?' Robyn said, daring to smile at the old tartar.

Mrs Soames's chin wobbled a bit and she cleared her throat. 'I've got the same room as last time,' she said.

Robyn checked her key. 'Oh, that's the Rose Room – it's lovely,' she said, remembering the pretty wallpaper covered in tiny rosebuds and the rich velvet curtains the colour of the deepest red rose.

'But I don't like the view,' Mrs Soames said.

Robyn did a double take. As far as she was concerned, there wasn't a single bad view from Purley Hall unless you didn't like country gardens, fields or woods. 'You don't like the view?' Robyn said, unable to disguise her bemusement.

'No. You can see the compost heap from there,' Mrs Soames told her.

'Oh,' Robyn said in surprise. 'Well, it probably isn't quite so big at this time of year. In fact, it's probably covered in snow.'

'A compost heap is a compost heap. It's rubbish. It's *waste*. And I haven't paid all this money to look out of my window to see waste.'

'Right,' Robyn said.

Doris Norris patted Robyn's arm. 'I rather like a compost heap,' she said. 'Maybe we could swap rooms.'

Mrs Soames looked suspicious for a moment as if Doris Norris might be up to something.

'Which room do you have?' Robyn asked her.

Doris looked down at her key. 'The Cedar Room,' she said.

'Oh, I had that one at my first conference,' Robyn said. 'It's gorgeous. It looks out over the front driveway and up into the cedar tree.'

'It won't be too noisy?' Mrs Soames asked.

'Oh, no,' Robyn said. 'You can keep an eye on everyone coming and going from there but it's lovely and quiet too,' she said, knowing how Mrs Soames liked to know everybody's business and would appreciate spying down on the world.

'Well, we'd better have a look then,' she said and the little group made their way to the Cedar Room.

Mrs Soames didn't give too much away when she entered the room but walked straight across the plush cream carpet to the sash window which looked out across the front driveway just as Robyn had promised.

'I suppose this will *have* to do,' she said at last and Robyn put her bags down with a sigh of relief.

'We'll see you for the welcome reception downstairs, then?' Robyn said, quickly leaving the room with Doris. 'It was very kind of you to swap rooms,' she said as she took Doris's suitcase to the Rose Room.

'If I can play my part in making Mrs Soames a little cheery then that's reward enough for me.'

'Well, she wasn't exactly smiling about it,' Robyn observed.

'No, I don't think I've ever seen her do anything but grimace,' Doris agreed. 'I've seen happier-looking bloodhounds.'

They giggled together.

'But you, my dear, you *do* look happy!' Doris continued as they reached the Rose Room.

Robyn smiled. 'I am,' she said.

'And this is your home now – with Dan?'

Robyn nodded. 'We've got a little cottage down the lane. It's tiny but perfect and I love working here with Dame Pamela.'

'I'm so glad you found the right man for you,' Doris said. 'I mean – after that fellow you were involved with.'

Robyn bit her lip as she remembered Jace and the time that they'd broken up during her first Jane Austen conference.

'Although I'll never forget him riding into the dining room on that horse!' Doris said.

Robyn shook her head at the memory. 'I got a Christmas card from him last week,' she said. 'He's just got engaged to a local girl. She likes pubs and football and I don't think she's an Austen fan so that will suit Jace wonderfully well.'

'That's nice – everyone deserves to find that special someone,' Doris said. 'Remember what Jane Austen said? "Do not be in a hurry: depend upon it -"'

'"The right man will come at last",' Robyn finished with her and Doris nodded in approval.

As the rest of the guests made themselves at home in their rooms, changing from snug travelling clothes into elegant dresses and smart trousers, Dame Pamela was pacing up and down her office. Every now and then, she would stop, pick up the phone and hit the 'redial' button but there was never any answer.

'Oh, Benedict!' she cried into the empty room before walking over to the bookcase. She reached up to a shelf just above her head and pulled out a thick photo album bound in leather with gilt lettering. She took it across to the desk and sat in the chair, flipping through the pages and staring at the photographs.

'So many brothers,' she said with a little laugh.

Depending on how you looked at it, her father had either been one of the world's worst philanderers or one of its greatest romantics. He had married four times and had had two other lovers who had given him children too. Dame Pamela often lost count of them all but she thought there were at least nine of them in total with her being the eldest and Dan being the youngest. Benedict was somewhere in the middle and was in his forties now but he still behaved like a teenager with his money-making schemes and his belief that a great fortune was owed to him without him actually having to work for it.

She looked at her favourite photo of him in the album. It had been taken on a holiday somewhere on the south coast. Dame Pamela had forgotten where. Her father had hired a huge house overlooking the sea and had filled the place with his children. It had been chaos but a wonderful sort of chaos.

She looked at the young boy in the photograph with his cheeky grin and mop of badly-behaved hair. What age would he have been there? Ten maybe eleven? Even then, he'd been trouble. Dame Pamela shook her head as she remembered Benedict marching up and down the beach trying to sell shells and stones to the tourists.

She turned the page and there was a photo of the two of them together, standing on the balcony of the holiday home, the brilliant blue sea behind them. She looked more like his mother than his sister and she'd been forced into that role through the years as Benedict had lurched from one financial disaster to the next.

'And what sort of trouble are you in now?' she asked the photograph before gazing out of the window into the white landscape beyond.

CHAPTER 5

Higgins the butler, who was sporting a cherry-red waistcoat with bright silver buttons, cleared his throat and a hush descended on the room as twenty pairs of eyes fixed themselves on the door.

'Ladies and gentlemen,' he began, 'Dame Pamela Harcourt.'

As ever, Dame Pamela entered the room like an empress and was greeted by much applause. She was wearing a pale gold dress draped with a crimson shawl and her hair was swept up and pinned with an enormous diamond clip. She was famous for her diamonds and there were gasps from the audience as she walked to the front of the room, her eyelashes batting as she drank in the adoration of her guests. Nobody would have guessed that, just ten minutes before, she'd been having a nervous breakdown in the privacy of her study. "The show must go on" was a phrase that every actress knew and Dame Pamela had lived her life by it.

She took a deep breath and began. 'I can't tell you what a delight it is to welcome you all here for our special Christmas conference! We've been discussing having one for some time now and I think it's particularly appropriate as it's also the month of Jane Austen's birthday.'

There was a cheer and Dame Pamela clutched a hand to her heart and her eyes rose towards heaven as if communing with the great author herself.

'So this conference is going to be *extra* special as we celebrate our favourite author's birthday. There will be the usual talks and readings and film showings, and we have some very special guests lined up for you. And, because this is Christmas, there will be plenty of food and drink but we will also have lots of dancing too so that our waistlines don't suffer *too* much!'

There was another round of applause and then Higgins got to work with the silver tray, distributing glasses of the cocktail which Dame Pamela had named the *Fitzwilliam Fizzer*. There was also a non-alcoholic alternative that Dame Pamela called a *Pink Bingley* but it wasn't proving quite as popular as the *Fitzwilliam Fizzer* but it got everybody talking about cocktails.

'I think a *Wicked Wickham* would slip down rather nicely,' Roberta told her sister Rose who had the good grace to blush at such a suggestion.

'What about a *Tickling Tilney*?' Doris Norris suggested.

'Or a *Wentworth Wallbanger*,' Roberta said.

Mrs Soames, who was in earshot, tutted loudly and sipped at her *Pink Bingley* without joining in with the chatter.

After circulating amongst her guests, Dame Pamela walked over to the window and looked out over the snow-covered garden to the fields beyond. She was thankful that her guests had had problem-free journeys and that everybody had arrived safely but there were two guests who hadn't arrived yet – the actress, Gemma Reilly, and the uninvited brother, Benedict Harcourt.

'Madam,' Higgins said, appearing by her side, 'I've just had a call from Master Benedict.'

'*Please* tell me he's been snowed in and can't possibly make it,' Dame Pamela said, knowing it was deeply uncharitable but quite unable to stop herself.

'I'm afraid not,' Higgins said. 'He just wanted to let you know that he'll be here in time for dinner.'

Dame Pamela sighed. 'He always did have an uncanny ability to arrive at precisely the wrong moment.'

But Benedict Harcourt didn't arrive in time for dinner and the guests enjoyed a carefree and very splendid meal by candlelight before the first evening's activities got under way. There was a showing of *Miss Austen Regrets* in the drawing room whilst Regency parlour games were on offer in the library.

Kay and Adam had chosen the parlour games but Adam had missed his cue at a game of cards twice now and Kay looked concerned as he checked his phone again.

'What is it?' she asked.

'It's Gemma – she's stuck somewhere outside London. I don't think she's going to make it tonight.'

'Oh, dear,' Kay said. 'Perhaps the roads will be better in the morning.'

Adam sighed. 'But our talk's at eleven o'clock.'

'She'll be here,' Kay said, reaching across the round table to squeeze his hand.

'I won't be able to do it without her,' he said, blinking hard behind his glasses.

'You'll be fine,' she told him but she knew that he'd rather walk naked through the snow than give a talk on his own in front of a room full of people.

Adam Craig was the sweetest man Kay had ever met but his crippling shyness had almost stopped them from getting together and Kay had actually believed him to be in love with Gemma the actress. When he'd walked into her bed and breakfast in Lyme Regis during the filming of *Persuasion*, she hadn't really noticed him at all because she'd had a big crush on the actor Oli Wade Owen. Well, what Janeite *wouldn't* fall in love with a handsome actor playing Captain Wentworth?

But sweet, kind Adam had been there for her when it had all gone wrong and she couldn't envisage them ever being apart now.

'Gemma will make it,' Kay told him again. 'She's a very determined woman.'

Adam nodded and took a deep breath. 'Okay.'

'And, if she doesn't make it, *I'll* do the talk with you.'

'Really?' Adam said, his eyes lighting up.

'You're forgetting that I lived through the whole film experience too,' she said.

He smiled at her. 'I could never forget that,' he said, leaning forward and kissing her.

They then proceeded to slay each other at piquet.

Later that night, after all the food had been eaten, all the drinks had been quaffed and all the card games played out, the guests at Purley Hall lay sleeping in their beds, unaware that the snow was falling thick and fast, smothering the landscape under a glistening white blanket.

In a pink and white bedroom at the back of Purley Hall, Dame Pamela was just dreaming about an actor she'd dated in her twenties called Piers Dalrymple when there was a faint tapping on the door.

'Madam?'

Dame Pamela groaned as she slowly began to wake up, leaving the arms of Piers Dalrymple and switching on her bedside lamp. It flooded the room with soft amber light.

'Higgins? Is that you?'

The door opened and Higgins stood there in his long paisley dressing gown. 'I'm sorry to disturb you, madam, but I think Master Benedict has arrived.'

Dame Pamela sat up in bed and yawned. Her hair was full of large curlers and her face was flushed with sleep.

'What time is it?'

'A little after three,' Higgins said.

'Oh, why couldn't he have arrived at a more civil sort of hour?' Dame Pamela said, swinging her legs out of bed. Higgins handed her the pink robe with the feather collar and she wrapped herself up in it, placing her feet a pair of cerise slippers which sparkled with sequins.

'I think, perhaps, that the snow impeded his journey,' Higgins said.

'Oh, I suppose so.'

'It's falling quite thickly now.'

Dame Pamela walked across to the window and peered out through the curtains and a swirl of snowflakes greeted her.

'We're going to be snowed in at this rate,' she said. 'I'm glad we bought all the food and drink we did.'

The two of them left the bedroom and walked along the corridor before heading down the staircase to the front door just as there was a loud rapping on it.

'Quick! Before he wakes up the entire house!' Dame Pamela whispered.

Higgins unlocked the great door and there, standing under the light of the porch lamp, was Benedict Harcourt, his round face red with cold.

He strode into the hallway and stamped his boots on the beautiful floor, leaving little piles of melted snow everywhere. Dame Pamela tried not to grimace and Higgins made a mental note to grab a mop at the earliest convenience.

'So good to see you, Pamsy!' Benedict said, dropping two suitcases down before stepping forward and squashing his sister in a hug. His coat was thick and wet with snow and instantly flattened Dame Pamela's feathery neckline.

'Benedict!' she cried. 'What a – *surprise!*'

'Ah! You know me – could never resist a surprise.'

'Indeed,' Dame Pamela said.

'And Christmas is the time for surprises!' he said, removing his woolly hat and shaking his hair. Droplets of snow sprayed outwards catching both Dame Pamela and Higgins.

Higgins was just about to lock the door when a slender figure appeared around it.

'Hello?' she said, her eyes blinking in the sudden brightness of the hallway light.

'Gemma?' Dame Pamela said, stepping forward.

Gemma removed her stripy hat and Dame Pamela hugged her, impervious now as to how bedraggled her feathers had become.

'Ah!' Benedict cried. 'This is the lovely lady who came to my rescue. My car broke down about five miles away and there was nobody about but then this dear soul turns up and blow me down if she wasn't heading for Purley!'

'I came in my four by four and it's a good job I did,' Gemma told Dame Pamela. 'Some of the roads are pretty much blocked now and we had to leave the car at the end of the driveway. I hope that's all right?'

'Oh, don't worry about that – come and get warm, for goodness' sake. Higgins – see if you can get the fire going again in the drawing room.'

'Yes, madam.'

'And some drinks.'

'Good idea, Pamsy! A whiskey – that marvellous single malt you have - would go down a treat.'

'I was thinking more of a hot chocolate,' Dame Pamela said.

Benedict's face filled with disappointment as he followed his sister into the drawing room and they sat down as Higgins got the fire going, his bare knees protruding from out of his dressing gown.

'I'm so thrilled you made it, Gemma,' Dame Pamela said. 'We were getting worried about you, weren't we, Higgins?'

'Yes, Madam.'

'All this snow! You *are* a brave soul!'

'I didn't want to miss this,' Gemma said, unwinding her scarf from her neck as the fire got going. 'I've heard so much about your gatherings and I've really been looking forward to it.'

'But I *must* take you to task first,' Dame Pamela said, tightening up a curler which had worked its way loose.

'Oh?'

'You're not acting anymore, are you?'

Gemma shook her head. 'No,' she said.

'After the performance you gave as Anne Elliot, I have to say that it's positively a crime!' Dame Pamela shook her head in disapproval.

Gemma gave a little smile. 'I guess acting just wasn't for me,' she said. 'I used to get so nervous.'

'But we *all* get nervous,' Dame Pamela said. 'That's what drives a great performance. It's when you start to relax that it all goes horribly wrong.'

'Yes but I was nervous all the time even when I wasn't performing. I'd get nervous just thinking about the next job and what I might have to do and what would happen if it all went wrong. I'd have nightmares and get myself so worked up that I couldn't think about anything else.'

'Oh, dear!' Dame Pamela said.

'I never get nervous,' Benedict chipped in, taking a hot chocolate from the silver tray that Higgins had brought into the room.

'No,' Dame Pamela said. 'You're always filled with total confidence that things will go your way.'

'I am indeed, Pamsy,' he said. 'Any chance of a splosh of brandy in this?'

Higgins glanced at Dame Pamela and she nodded in consent.

'Anyway, I'm much happier doing what I'm doing now,' Gemma said.

'Yes, how is the shop?' Dame Pamela asked, remembering that Gemma's handmade knitted clothes for children had become instant bestsellers as soon as they'd gone on sale.

'It's doing really well,' Gemma said.

'In Marylebone High Street, isn't it?'

Gemma nodded. 'We're hoping to open another one in Wimbledon soon.'

'There's a chap in Wimbledon that owes me money,' Benedict said.

Dame Pamela's eyes widened. 'I expect a lot of people owe you money,' she said.

'You're damned right, sis,' he said, reaching for the brandy bottle which Higgins had left within arm's reach of Benedict. Dame Pamela frowned in disapproval.

They chatted away for half an hour or so, the fire crackling and the clock ticking above the mantelpiece.

Finally, believing that it would be most unseemly to yawn in front of her guests, Dame Pamela stood up.

'Well, I think it's time to call it a night,' she said. 'Higgins will see you to your rooms. Good night.' She kissed them both and left them in the capable hands of her butler before returning to her bedroom.

As she climbed back into bed, Dame Pamela thought what a great relief it was that Gemma had arrived but she was still concerned about her brother and guessed that only time would tell the truth about his reason for visiting Purley Hall.

CHAPTER 6

A white world greeted the guests the next morning. Mia Castle was one of the first out of bed and whipped the curtains back, blinding her poor sister.

'Sarah!' she cried. 'Come and see!'

Sarah sat up in bed and blinked in the bright white light that flooded the bedroom.

'Come *on!* Mia pleaded as if all the snow might suddenly melt away.

Sarah brushed her hair out of her face and placed her feet into her slippers – first the left and then the right, careful not to touch the carpet – and joined her sister at the window.

'Oh!' she said as she saw the sight that greeted her. Their bedroom was at the back of the house overlooking the garden and the landscape beyond and everything had turned white. It was the softest, sparkliest, dreamiest of worlds. The ground was covered in at least six inches of snow and all the trees were wearing white garments. The garden obelisks had turned from hard stone to soft wool and the lake had disappeared completely.

Mia opened the sash window and leaned out. 'Listen. Isn't it quiet? I love that about snow. It seems to absorb all sound.'

Sarah nodded and then shivered. 'We'd better get ready for breakfast,' she said, moving away from the window.

Mia closed it with a sigh. 'It's going to be a white Christmas,' she said with a laugh. 'Sarah?'

'Yes?'

'Are you okay?'

Sarah turned around to look at Mia. 'Of course,' she said.

'You seem quiet.'

'Next to you, *everyone's* quiet,' Sarah said with a little smile.

'I know but you're even quieter than usual.' Concern was etched across Mia's face. 'Everything okay?'

'Yes,' Sarah said but Mia could see that she was hiding something. She was the world's worst liar.

'Sure?'

'Yes,' Sarah said. 'Now, let's get ready for breakfast.'

Half an hour later, the sisters walked down the grand staircase and entered the dining room for breakfast. A side table had been set out with glasses, cups and plates, and guests were helping themselves to fruit juice, cereal, toast and croissants before ordering cooked breakfasts.

'Who's that man?' Mia asked.

Sarah looked up from where she was choosing a glass which didn't have any smears on it. 'The one by the window?'

Mia nodded. The man was in his late forties and was tall and thin with dark hair and a moustache that might have looked sexy on Errol Flynn but which looked horribly suspicious hovering on his face.

'I've no idea,' Sarah said.

'I've not noticed him before but he kind of stands out, doesn't he?'

They took their breakfast over to the table and sat down just as the man turned around from the window.

'Good morning,' he said with a tight smile as he sat down next to Mia. 'I'm Jackson Moore.'

'I'm Mia and this is my sister, Sarah,' Mia said.

He nodded and stroked his strange moustache with his long, tapering fingers. 'And you're both Austen fans, are you?'

Mia gave him a startled look as if to say what a silly question that was.

'We are indeed,' Sarah said, tapping her sister's foot with her own under the table in an attempt to remind her of the importance of manners.

'And you must be too?' Mia said.

'Well, of course,' he said.

'And what's your favourite book?' Mia asked, feeling the weight of Sarah's foot on hers once again as if her sister knew she was testing him.

'*Pride and Prejudice*, of course,' he said. 'Isn't that everybody's favourite?'

'Not at all,' Mia said, her voice filled with annoyance. '*Our* favourite is *Sense and Sensibility*.'

Jackson Moore nodded sagely and Mia turned away from him to get on with her breakfast and he eventually stood up and left the room.

'Mia!' Sarah whispered. 'Why were you so abrupt with him?'

'Because I don't like him,' Mia said matter-of-factly.

'But you were so rude,' Sarah said.

'I don't care. He wasn't–' Mia paused.

'What?'

'Right. He wasn't right!'

'Because he was a man?'

'No, not because he was a man. He's just odd.'

'Well, he doesn't seem like your typical Janeite but who are we to say who can and can't admire Jane Austen?'

Mia shook her head. 'I just didn't believe him,' she said.

'Your trouble is you're too judgemental. You jump to conclusions and don't give people a chance. He's probably some poor widower who might not be able to tell Captain Wentworth from General Tilney but is just as fascinated by the books as we are.'

Mia made a funny sort of scoffing noise. 'We'll see,' she said.

In the West Drawing Room, Adam and Gemma were getting ready for their presentation.

'Thank goodness you're here!' Adam told Gemma as she arranged her notes on the little table between their two chairs. 'I was so worried about you last night.'

'Worried that you'd have to do the talk on your own?' she teased.

Adam flushed red. 'Well, yes,' he said, 'but worried that you were stuck somewhere too.'

'I nearly did get stuck,' she said, 'and I'm guessing we're all snowed in here for a while.'

'I can think of worse fates,' Adam said. 'Did Rob not fancy coming with you?' he asked, remembering Gemma's new husband whom she'd met on the set of *Persuasion*.

'Oh, this isn't his sort of thing at all,' Gemma said. 'Anyway, he's got one of his brothers over from Ireland. They're going to sit and drink whiskey and talk into the small hours without any interruption from me.'

'And how's your mother?' Adam asked, remembering Gemma's famous actress mother, Kim Reilly, who'd been a big star in the seventies hit show *Bandits*.

'Oh, she's fine,' Gemma said. 'Actually, she's working on her first screenplay.'

'Really? I didn't know your mother wrote. I mean, she doesn't strike me as the writerly type.'

'Well, she's written the biggest part with herself in mind,' Gemma said with a grin. 'And she asked me if I'd give you a copy of the first draft. I said no, of course, but you know what she's like. She absolutely insisted so I've brought it with me but don't feel you have to, Adam. It's really overstepping the mark.'

'No, no,' Adam assured her. 'I'll take a look at it.'

'You will?'

'Of course I will.'

'And handle her with care?' Gemma said.

'Absolutely.'

'Because you know what she can be like.'

'Indeed I do,' he said, remembering the affection-craving actress he'd met on the set of *Persuasion* and how she'd made poor Gemma's life a total nightmare.

'Thanks so much, Adam,' Gemma said. 'I really appreciate it.'

'You're welcome.'

The drawing room door opened and the first of the guests walked in, taking their seats before Adam had the chance to run away.

'Just keep breathing,' Gemma whispered to him and he nodded, pushing his glasses up his nose like a nervous teacher before a class of students.

Kay was one of the first in and took a seat in the front row. 'Are you okay?' she asked Adam. He nodded again but she could see the look of panic in his eyes. 'Just remember that everyone loves everything you do!'

Adam took a deep breath as the rest of the seats filled up. It was time to begin.

After telling the audience how he'd come to be such a big Jane Austen fan and how his love of his native Lyme Regis had encouraged him to write and produce an adaptation of *Persuasion*, Gemma explained how she went about portraying the film's heroine, Anne Elliot.

The talk was illustrated with numerous photographs taken during the production and the ones of Oli Wade Owen dressed as Captain Wentworth went down particularly well with the ladies.

It was then time for questions from the audience.

'What was it like kissing Oli Wade Owen?' Doris Norris asked with a little giggle.

'Ah, but I didn't,' Gemma said. 'Anne Elliot kissed Captain Wentworth and it was pretty wonderful.'

Everyone laughed.

'Will either of you do more Austen adaptations?' Roberta asked from the second row.

Gemma was the first to answer. 'I'm not acting anymore, I'm afraid, so I won't be. But Adam – you're working on something at the moment, aren't you?'

'Well, yes. It's very early days but I've got a modern adaptation of *Sense and Sensibility* under way and I'm hoping we'll be able to shoot it in Devon next year.'

This news was greeted with much approval and Mia nudged Sarah. 'It's probably our life story,' she said.

'I doubt it,' Sarah said with a little smile. 'It would be deemed highly implausible!'

After lunch, there was a talk by another of the guests – Doctor Katherine Roberts from St Bridget's College in Oxford. A happy hour was spent discussing the role of mothers in the novels of Jane Austen and it was concluded that they were a pretty bad bunch on the whole although it was agreed that Mrs Dashwood from *Sense and Sensibility* was the most likeable and had done her very best for her daughters.

There was then an afternoon showing of the recent BBC adaptation of *Emma* and everybody cheered whenever snow was seen. There were also a couple of naughty wolf whistles for Jonny Lee Miller's Mr Knightley too and, as usual amongst Jane Austen fans, a conversation ensued about who was the best Mr Knightley.

'I rather preferred Jeremy Northam as Mr Knightley,' Doris Norris said.

Rose shook her head. 'He was far too gentle. He practically bordered on the effeminate. Mark Strong was *much* better.'

'I'd like to see Richard Armitage as Mr Knightley,' Roberta said with a little sigh.

'I'd like to see Richard Armitage in anything,' Doris Norris said. 'Or nothing!' she added and the three of them chuckled

'Shush!' Mrs Soames hissed from the front row. '*Some* of us are trying to watch this!'

CHAPTER 7

Whilst most of the guests were wallowing in *Emma*, Dame Pamela was in her office with Higgins.

'I must say, I'm rather nervous about this, Higgins,' she said.

'I'm not surprised, madam,' he said.

'I've been looking forward to it so much but, now the time is approaching, I feel all fluttery!' She gave a girlish laugh, her hand flying to the pearl choker around her neck.

Higgins cleared his throat which was always a sign that he had something to say although he'd never venture an opinion without being invited to.

'What is it, Higgins?' Dame Pamela asked, looking at her faithful butler and noticing that he looked decidedly twitchy.

'If I may say something, madam?' he said, eyebrows arching imperiously.

'Of course.'

He cleared his throat again which made Dame Pamela even more anxious to hear what he had to say.

'We don't really know these people,' he said.

'What do you mean?' she asked.

'I mean that what you're about to do – what you're about to show them-'

'What?'

'It seems rather risky to me,' he said.

'How can you say that?' Dame Pamela asked. 'These people are all Jane Austen fans and that makes us like family!'

'But they're not family.'

'Look, Higgins, I've worked with countless people in my profession. I've met some gems and I've met some real stinkers too and I like to think that I'm a pretty good judge of character and there's not one guest here that I wouldn't trust with my life. Well, as long as we keep an eye on

Benedict, that is. Just in case he decides to run away with it.'

Higgins nodded as if in agreement. 'And you'll make sure you'll return it to the safe afterwards?' he said.

'Of course I will. Really, Higgins, I do think you're worrying about nothing.'

'One should always remain cautious,' he said. 'Best safety lies in fear.'

Dame Pamela blinked in surprise. 'I didn't know you knew *Hamlet*,' she said.

'I have been known to read the Bard on occasion,' Higgins said, giving a little nod of his head before leaving the room.

'Hey!' Dan said as he entered the kitchen. 'I've been looking all over for you. I thought you were watching *Emma*.'

Robyn looked up from the rocking chair where she was holding a sleeping Cassandra, her long corkscrew curls tickling her daughter's head. 'I was but Cassie started getting grouchy. I think she wanted her nap so we came down here for a while.'

'It's certainly the place to be,' Dan said, kissing Robyn before pulling up a wooden chair and joining her by the AGA whose heat was filling the room. 'I've just been outside and it's absolutely freezing. The drive's completely covered and it looks like we're all snowed in for the next few days.'

'Good job nobody's planning on going anywhere then, isn't it?'

Dan nodded. 'I'm glad I brought Moby and Biscuit with me this morning but we'll have to nip back to the cottage to feed the hens . Pammy's said we can stay in the attic room. Higgins is making sure it's all ship-shape. She didn't want to put us all the way up there but all the other rooms are full.'

'The attic room's fine. Is the rocking horse still up there?'

Dan nodded. 'I can give Cassie her first riding lesson.'

Robyn smiled. Dan had been talking about getting Cassie into the saddle since she'd been born but Robyn insisted on waiting until she started school. 'That'll be soon enough,' she'd told him.

They sat in comfortable silence for a few minutes, watching Cassie as she slept. Robyn stroked her red-gold hair. She'd inherited her father's colouring although it had a tendency to curl like Robyn's hair.

'How are things going with Benedict?' Robyn asked at last.

'I've left him in the drawing room. He's smoking his way through Higgins's cigars.'

'And you haven't found out why he's here?'

'He keeps talking about the "spirit of Christmas",' Dan said, 'but I don't believe him. He's never been the sort to put a family Christmas first. He's hiding something, all right, but I haven't winkled it out of him yet.'

'He seems nice enough,' Robyn said.

'Oh, he's always been an affable sort.'

Robyn grinned.

'What?' Dan asked her.

'You said *affable*,' she said.

'What's wrong with that?'

'Nothing!' she said. 'But you're beginning to sound like a Janeite.'

Dan grinned. 'I'm not surprised,' he said. 'You can't move around Purley these days without being assaulted by *affables* and *amiables*.'

Robyn laughed. 'I think it's something we're going to have to get used to with all these conferences.'

'Yes, Pammy shows no signs of slowing down or thinking about retirement anytime soon.'

'I'm glad to hear it,' Robyn said, 'otherwise I'd be out of a job.'

'Oh, I don't think so,' Dan said. 'If Pammy ever does retire, I'm sure you'd be running these conferences yourself.'

'You think she'd keep them going?'

'Are you kidding? Pammy *adores* having a house full of people. She'll never give that up even when she reaches a hundred - which I'm sure she will.'

Robyn smiled. 'You're right,' she said. 'Now, how do you fancy keeping an eye on Cassandra for a while?'

'Sure,' Dan said, taking the sleeping baby from his wife. 'What are you up to?'

'I've just *got* to pop back and watch the end of *Emma*. I *can't* miss that proposal scene in the garden!'

After Mr Knightley had kissed Emma Woodhouse to rapturous applause, it was time to get ready for dinner.

Katherine had been chatting to Robyn after the showing of *Emma* and, realising the time, dashed up the stairs to get changed. Entering the bedroom, she saw Warwick stooped over his suitcase, hunting through the clothes and books he'd packed.

'Warwick? What are you looking for?' she asked.

He jumped and span around. 'Oh, you startled me!' he said.

'Have you lost something?'

'No!'

'You looked as if you were searching for something,' she said, suspicion in her voice.

'No, no. Not to worry,' he said, straightening his jacket.

Katherine nodded and then walked across to the window. It had been dark for hours but the falling snow was still visible in the light thrown out from the windows.

'How on earth are we all to get home?' she said.

Warwick came and stood behind her, pushing her long dark hair aside and kissing her neck. 'We've only just arrived!' he said.

'I know but-'

'But nothing,' he said, turning her around to face him. 'Don't worry about the journey home or the state of the roads or if we'll have to dig the car out by hand and push it all the way back to Sussex.' He kissed the tip of her nose.

'I wasn't worrying,' she told him. 'At least, I wasn't worrying until you said all those things. I was merely thinking that I've never seen so much snow and-'

'And wouldn't it be wonderful if we got snowed in at Purley Hall and had to stay forever and ever,' Warwick interrupted.

'Well, it might be wonderful for a little while but we've both got to get back and write our books and I've got students to teach and my neighbour really can't be expected to look after Freddie and Fitz forever,' Katherine said.

Warwick stopped her mouth with a kiss. 'Your cats will be fine. Your students will be fine. But *I* won't be fine if you don't give me one hundred percent of your attention right now.'

Katherine smiled, took a deep breath and then obliged him.

The dining room looked magical. The fire was roaring and all the candelabra had been lit. The women glittered in dresses bejewelled with beads and sequins and the men looked resplendent in crisp shirts and waistcoats.

Dinner was eaten to the sound of gentle chatter and, after the main course was finished, a great cake was wheeled into the dining room. It was three tiers high and a delicate pink and was lit with forty-one candles to mark the age of Jane Austen when she'd died.

There was plenty for everyone to have seconds and even thirds and it was all washed down with champagne and a special toast to celebrate Jane Austen's birthday.

'Don't drink too much, Mia,' Sarah warned her sister. 'We need to keep our minds sharp for the quiz this evening.'

'There can't *possibly* be any questions I won't know the answer to. I'm a walking encyclopaedia when it comes to Jane Austen,' Mia boasted.

'You might be surprised,' Sarah said. 'I've heard the quiz can be surprisingly tough.'

CHAPTER 8

'Into groups! Into groups!' Dame Pamela chorused, clapping her hands together and sending a thousand sparks shooting around the library from her diamond rings.

The guests quickly got themselves into little groups around tables that had been laid out with after dinner mints and sheets of pretty note paper and pens. Doris Norris joined sisters Roberta and Rose, Gemma joined Adam and Kay, and Robyn and Dan joined Katherine and Warwick.

'Everybody knows that I adore a quiz!' Dame Pamela began, standing to the left of the great fireplace, 'and this is a special Christmas-themed quiz.'

A cheer went up in the library.

'And there's a special Christmas prize too. A beautiful set of hampers from Fortnum and Mason filled with Christmas goodies.'

Necks craned to get a look at the prize.

'And runners up prizes of signed photographs of me as Lady Catherine de Bourgh in *Pride and Prejudice.*'

'A hamper's more use,' Mrs Soames said to her neighbour.

'So, let the quiz commence!' Dame Pamela said. 'Question number one. Janeites have another reason to celebrate the Christmas season because it marks Jane Austen's birthday but what was the *exact* date of her birth?'

Katherine and Robyn exchanged glances as if to say that no question could be easier for an Austen fan, for who wasn't aware of when their idol had came into the world?

'The sixteenth of December 1775,' Warwick whispered.

'Of course,' Katherine said, writing the answer down in her neat script with a fountain pen that Warwick had bought for her for her last birthday. He'd had it engraved with the words 'so much in love' which was a quotation from *Pride and Prejudice* and Katherine loved it dearly.

'Next question,' Dame Pamela said, 'it's a quote and I want to know who wrote it and whom they wrote it to. Ready? "You are all to come to Pemberley at Christmas."'

'Oh!' Dan said. 'That's from-'

Robyn hushed him. 'Don't give answers away to the opposition!' she warned him.

'But that's from *Pride and Prejudice*,' he said excitedly.

Robyn smiled across at Katherine and Warwick. 'That's the only Austen novel he's read,' she explained, nudging him gently in the ribs.

'Okay, then,' Katherine said. 'Who said it, Dan?'

'Well, I don't know that much,' he admitted.

'It's Elizabeth,' Robyn said. 'It's right at the end in a letter she writes to the Gardiners.'

Katherine nodded in agreement and wrote it down.

'A tough one now,' Dame Pamela said. 'In the winter of what year did Jane Austen receive a marriage of proposal from Harris Bigg-Wither?'

There was a ripple of laughter around the room as there always was at the mention of his name.

Warwick took a deep breath. 'Well, I'm stumped.'

'It must have been the early eighteen hundreds,' Robyn said. 'Eighteen-'

'1802,' Katherine finished.

'Give Robyn a chance!' Warwick said. 'She was probably going to say that.'

'Actually, I was going to say 1803,' Robyn confessed.

'That might be right,' Warwick said.

'It's 1802,' Katherine said. 'Trust me.'

'Ready for the next question?' Dame Pamela asked. 'Which festive drink in the eighteenth-century was made from arrack, water, lemon juice, sugar and spices?'

'Warwick?' Katherine said, pointing her fountain pen at him.

'Why would I know the answer to that?' he said.

'Because you're known to like a tipple!'

'Oh, all right – it's punch,' he said with a grin.

'Next question,' Dame Pamela said. 'In *Emma*, who was – and I quote – "snowed up at a friend's house once for a week"?'

'Oh, it's that odious Mr Elton,' Robyn said. 'His poor friends have to endure him for a *whole* week! Can you imagine.'

'Could be worse,' Warwick announced. 'Could've been Mr Collins.'

Robyn nodded. 'Imagine having to entertain *both* of them at once. Wouldn't that be awful?'

'They'd probably absolutely adore each other,' Warwick said.

'I don't think they would,' Katherine said. 'I think Mr Collins would probably feel threatened by Mr Elton.'

There was no time to discuss the fictional meeting between these two literary anti-heroes any longer for Dame Pamela was ready with the next question.

The library clock ticked and chimed each quarter hour and the fire crackled as the questions came thick and fast. Finally, it was time for the last question.

'Which novel paints this Christmas scene?' Dame Pamela paused and then began the quote: "On one side was a table occupied by some chattering girls, cutting up silk and gold paper and on the other were tressels and trays, bending under the weight of brawn and cold pies."'

'It's *Persuasion*,' Katherine said.

'Are you sure it's not *Emma*?' Warwick asked.

Katherine shook her head. 'No, it's definitely *Persuasion*.'

'Boy, am I glad you're on our team,' Warwick said, picking up her hand and squeezing it.

'Well, I'm afraid I wasn't much use,' Dan said with an apologetic smile.

'You just need to read a few more of the novels,' Robyn told him.

'Don't forget to put your group's name on the top of your answers,' Dame Pamela said, 'and coffee will be served as the answers are being marked.'

'Oh, what shall we call ourselves?' Robyn said.

'We could use "Bennets and Bonnets" again,' Warwick said.

'But Dan's new to our group this time,' Robyn said. 'We should have a new name.'

They sat mulling it over for a moment.

'Snow and Snowibility?' Dan suggested.

They laughed.

'That's not bad,' Warwick said.

'There you go – at least I was good for something!' Dan said.

Robyn kissed him on the cheek and stood up. 'I'm just going to check on Cassie. We shouldn't leave your poor brother with her *all* evening.'

Benedict Harcourt looked very much at home in the West Drawing Room with Cassie in his arms.

'How are you getting on?' Robyn asked him as she entered the room.

He smiled up at Robyn and ruffled his hair. Like Dan and Cassie's, it was a red-gold and was positively glowing in the lamp light as were his cheeks but Robyn assumed that that was from the tumbler of whiskey he'd been drinking.

'We've been getting on famously!' he said, squeezing Cassie's tiny body.

'Well, I can't thank you enough for keeping an eye on her.'

'How did the quiz go? Did you win?' he asked.

'We'll find out in a few minutes. I'll just pop this one to bed first.'

'Want a hand? I can carry her upstairs if you like.'

'Oh, that would be kind.'

'It would be my pleasure,' Benedict said, standing up with Cassie in his arms.

They walked up the great staircase together and Robyn couldn't help noticing that Benedict was smiling.

'What is it?' she asked him.

'I was just thinking that I used to carry little Dan to bed like this.'

Robyn smiled. It wasn't often that she heard her tall husband described as 'little' and she tried to imagine the scene with the two brothers.

'We didn't get much time together with such a huge age gap, though,' he said. 'I just got to see him on the occasional family holiday and the rare family Christmas.'

'And is that why you're here now? To spend more time with the family?'

'It is indeed,' he said as they reached the attic room. Robyn waited for him to say more but he didn't and she watched as he placed Cassie in the little cot next to the rocking horse. 'Good heavens!' he said as he saw it. 'It's old Cinnamon!'

'He's rather magnificent, isn't he?' Robyn said as she tucked Cassie into bed, stroking her hair. 'Your sister said we can have him at Horseshoe Cottage but I can't bear to move him. He looks so at home here.'

Benedict gave the rocking horse a friendly pat. 'Dad bought this for Gervaise,' he said.

Robyn nodded. Gervaise was yet another of Dan's brothers she hadn't had the pleasure of meeting. He was the businessman who was always flying off to destinations Robyn had never heard of.

'Ah, he loved this horse!' Benedict said and Robyn felt sure she could see tears swimming in his eyes. But he quickly shook his head, as if dispelling the past. 'Right, let's get back to that whiskey,' he said.

Robyn made it back down to the library just in time to hear the winners of the quiz announced.

'With an astonishing twenty out of twenty,' Dame Pamela said, 'it's "Mr Darcy's Pride!"'

'Who's that?' Robyn asked.

'It's dear Doris Norris!' Katherine said.

Everybody applauded and Doris Norris, together with Rose and Roberta, went to collect their Christmas hampers.

'I can't believe we didn't win,' Dan said.

'I'm afraid we just can't compete with the likes of Doris!' Katherine said.

'Badly done, Katherine!' Warwick said and received an elbow in his ribs.

'And, in second place, it's Snow and Snowibility,' Dame Pamela announced.

'So we all win a signed photo of my dear sister?' Dan said as everybody applauded them.

Warwick grinned. 'Just what you've always wanted, eh, Dan?'

That night, once he was quite sure Katherine was asleep, Warwick got out of bed and, using the light from his mobile phone, searched through his suitcase once again.

'Damn it!' he cursed as he caught his finger on a notebook and gave himself a paper cut. As if he didn't have enough of those already, he thought. Now, where was it? He was quite sure he'd put it in the little zipped compartment but it wasn't there now. Maybe he'd imagined it. Maybe he hadn't packed it at all which would put a real dampener on his plans because he couldn't –

Katherine stirred and Warwick turned the light off on his phone until he could hear the gentle rhythm of her breathing again and knew she was asleep. Once more, he turned the light on and hunted through his clothes again but it definitely wasn't there. Defeated, he returned to bed, staring up into the darkness and praying to the saint of lost things that it was in a safe place somewhere back at The Old Vicarage.

Getting back into bed, he sighed, unaware that Katherine wasn't asleep at all. She'd heard Warwick get out of bed and search through his case, yet again, and had only been feigning sleep when he'd turned his light off.

What had Warwick been doing? He'd kept a secret from her once before and she didn't like the idea that he was hiding something else from her now.

CHAPTER 9

When Robyn opened her eyes the next morning, the first thing she saw was snow. It had settled on the sloping attic window and she gazed up into the myriad of glistening flakes.

'Dan?' she whispered, turning over in bed and squeezing his bare shoulder.

He blinked an eye open. 'Cassie?'

'She's still asleep,' Robyn said, remembering how he'd got up in the night each time she'd woken for her feed. He'd then cuddled and comforted her until she'd gone back to sleep. He'd then got back into bed and cuddled and comforted Robyn.

'Look at the snow on the window,' Robyn said.

Dan rolled over and gazed upwards, a smile waking up on his face. 'It's like being in an igloo,' he said, wrapping his arms around Robyn.

They gazed up at the snow together for a few minutes before Robyn sighed. 'We should get up.'

'Do we have to? We could stay cosied up like this all day? It is Christmas Eve, after all.'

'But it's going to be a very special day, remember?'

Dan frowned. 'Oh, you mean the big surprise?'

'Pamela wouldn't even tell me what it was. She's been planning it for weeks and I've no idea what it is. I walked into the office a few weeks ago and she was up to something. She was on the phone to somebody and hung up as soon as I walked in.'

'What do you think it could be?'

'I have no idea but she's pretty excited about it,' Robyn said reluctantly pulling herself away from Dan's arms and getting out of bed to wake Cassie.

The three of them then got washed and dressed, using a tiny bathroom along the landing that looked as if it had last been used in the nineteen-fifties.

'Have you seen my watch?' Dan asked as they were about to go downstairs for breakfast.

'Your gold one?' Robyn said.

'Yes. The one Pammy bought me last Christmas.'

Robyn glanced around the room. 'When did you last see it?'

'I thought I put it on the bedside table before going to dinner last night.'

'Why weren't you wearing it?' Robyn asked.

'It kept catching on my shirt sleeve so I took it off,' Dan said.

'Have you looked in the drawer?'

'I've looked everywhere,' he said.

For one awful moment, Robyn was about to tell Dan that Benedict had been in their room the night before but surely he wouldn't have taken the watch.

'I'm sure it will turn up,' she said, and the three of them went downstairs to breakfast.

Mia watched as Sarah darted around the room like a busy bee, straightening the curtains, the bedding and even a portrait on the wall above the dressing table which wasn't in the least bit crooked. She was quite used to her sister's ways, of course, but there was something different about her this time.

'Sarah!' Mia cried, looking at her watch. 'Come on!'

'What?' Sarah looked up with a startled expression on her face as if she'd genuinely forgotten where she was and whom she was with.

'It's time for breakfast – remember?'

Sarah sat down in the little armchair by the window, looking defeated. 'Oh,' she said.

Mia's forehead crinkled with worry. 'What is it? What's wrong?' She walked across the room and perched on the window seat next to her sister. 'You've been acting strangely ever since we got here.'

'No I haven't!'

'Yes you have,' Mia insisted.

'No I haven't.'

Mia sighed. 'Okay, no you haven't been acting strangely since we got here. You've been acting strangely since we left home!'

'I have not!' Sarah insisted, determining to get up again but Mia grabbed her arm and stopped her.

'Why won't you talk to me?'

'Because there's nothing to talk about,' Sarah said.

'That's not true,' Mia said. 'I can tell when something's bothering you – your OCD gets completely out of control and you turn into some kind of whirling dervish. You can't hide from me. Something's wrong, isn't it?'

Sarah bit her lip and looked at her sister, knowing it was futile to try and hide the truth from her any longer. 'I'm pregnant,' she said at last.

Mia's eyes widened in delight. 'Really? Since when?'

'Since Lloyd took me for a weekend in Lyme Regis.'

'Oh, that's so romantic!'

Sarah nodded. 'He knows how much I adore Lyme and he loves it too and we had such a lovely time. We just walked around together, looking at all the old buildings and eating ice cream on the Cobb. But I didn't plan on getting pregnant. I mean, we were kind of trying but it's so early for us. I didn't expect-' she paused.

'What?' Mia asked.

'It's all happening so quickly. I don't know if I'm ready.'

'Nobody thinks they're ready, Sarah. Nobody *can* be ready - not really - because it's such a huge thing to happen.' Mia laughed. 'And I don't mean to scare you because it's the most wonderful thing in the world to happen. You've just got to give in to it and go along for the ride.'

'But I've *never* given in to anything. I've always been in control,' Sarah said.

'Yes, I know, but you're not in control now. That little person growing inside you is in control and you've got to take a back seat,' Mia told her. 'I know that's going to be really hard for you but it's the only way you'll get through all this and keep sane.'

'I don't know if I can do that,' Sarah said, her shoulders sagging.

'Of *course* you can. If *I* can do it, you most certainly can!'

'But motherhood is different for you,' Sarah said. 'You're a natural.'

'But you will be too,' Mia said.

'No, I won't. I'll be terrible!'

'Of course you won't be. You can't be any worse than me. You've seen the chaos I live in.'

Sarah nodded, thinking of the little terrace in Bath she shared with Gabe and how it had been transformed from a neat bachelor pad into a toddler's paradise since Mia had descended with little William.

'Exactly my point,' Sarah said. 'You like chaos. Chaos suits you but it doesn't suit me. I don't know if I'm really cut out to be a mother.'

'Sarah – you'll be a brilliant mother!' Mia assured her.

She shook her head. 'But how will I cope with all the mess? A baby is messy, isn't it?'

'Yes, but with you and Lloyd as parents, it's bound to be born with OCD already built in. It will probably be the tidiest baby in the world.'

'You think so?'

Mia nodded. 'It'll be changing its own nappy and have the house all set to rights before you and Lloyd are even out of bed in the morning.'

Sarah laughed.

Mia rested her head upon her sister's shoulder. 'Do you know if it's a boy or girl yet?'

'No,' Sarah said.

'Are you going to find out?'

'No. We've decided to wait.'

'And have you got any names in mind?'

Sarah sighed. 'Oh, yes,' she said.

'Let me guess – Elinor for a girl and Edward for a boy.'

'How did you guess?' Sarah asked in amazement.

Mia laughed. 'Well, it wasn't exactly rocket science! Does Lloyd approve?'

'He'd be happy with any name, I think. I could call it Lydia or Wickham and he wouldn't bat an eyelid.'

'You're going to be great parents,' Mia said.

'And you're going to be a great aunt,' Sarah said.

Mia smiled and Sarah knew exactly what she was thinking. 'Just like Jane Austen,' she said and Sarah nodded.

Katherine was late getting up. It made a nice change from her college timetable with her early morning starts, driving through the Oxfordshire countryside and then walking through the streets of Oxford to St Bridget's College.

'What's it looking like out there?' she asked from the deep, warm folds of bedding as Warwick drew the thick red and gold curtains back.

'Deep and crisp and even,' he said. 'The perfect Christmas Eve.'

'Come back to bed!'

'I've just got to write something down.'

Katherine sighed. Warwick was like a jack-in-the-box when he was writing the first draft of a novel. Meals were interrupted, phone calls were cut short and he'd be in and out of bed several times a night sometimes.

She watched as he reached for a notebook and scribbled something down in his scratchy handwriting that she frequently made fun of.

'You really should've become a doctor with your handwriting,' she teased.

'As long as *I* can read it,' he said, closing the notebook a moment later. 'Okay, what's on the programme this morning?'

'I suppose it's too cold for the "Undressing Mr Darcy" session, isn't it?' Katherine said.

Warwick grinned at her. 'Probably but you might be in luck because I hear there's an "Undressing Warwick Lawton" show instead.'

'Oh, really?' Katherine said with an arched eyebrow.

'Yep!' he said, slowly peeling off the jumper he'd put on for his early morning writing session. 'Only this session is for an audience of just one.'

'Let me think,' Katherine said. 'Can Warwick Lawton possibly compete with Mr Darcy?'

Warwick strode across the room and leapt into bed beside Katherine. 'You're forgetting something very important,' he said.

'What's that?'

'Mr Darcy can't do this to you.' And with that, he kissed her for a very long time indeed.

After breakfast, there was a demonstration on bonnet trimming in the library and everyone was given their very own bonnet - even the men. Dame Pamela had arranged the most gorgeous array of ribbons, feathers, artificial flowers and fruit including grapes, cherries, plums and apricots – just the fruits Jane Austen had once noted in a letter to her sister, Cassandra. Indeed, every Janeite in the room picked up on this immediately and started quoting 'flowers are very much worn and fruit is still more the thing'.

There was a bit of a scrum for the prettiest pieces of ribbon with the sky-blue, rose-pink and purple being the most popular. There was also some very pretty pieces of lace and, once everybody had gathered everything they needed, the serious task of bonnet trimming began.

It had to be said that there were some members of the group who seemed born to trim a bonnet and others who struggled. Doris Norris was a natural with a needle and thread and her little bonnet was blooming with a pretty cluster of flowers in next to no time whereas Mrs Soames was definitely struggling, her large fingers causing her to curse. At one point, she turned as red as the strawberry she was trying to sew onto her bonnet and the tutor had to step in before she did irreparable damage.

Sarah's bonnet was an elegant, understated masterpiece of green ribbon and red and gold flowers whereas Mia had crammed as much as possible onto hers.

'Your head can't possibly support all that fruit,' Sarah warned her.

'But I can't bear to choose between any of it. It's *all* so gorgeous!'

And Warwick was doing very well indeed until he came to do a ruffled ribbon trim and then he became all fingers and thumbs. Even Jackson Moore was having a go but he wasn't as calm-headed as Warwick and kept cursing under his breath and twitching his moustache as he dropped all of his strawberries and then several cherries on the floor.

Finally, after everyone had finished, a central aisle was cleared and a mini fashion show was held with everyone modelling their bonnets to great applause. Dame Pamela then declared Mia the winner.

'For her wit and ambition in using every *possible* ingredient on her bonnet!' Her prize was a book about Regency costume full of exquisite illustrations. Mia was delighted and couldn't resist teasing Sarah who was still of the opinion that her sister's bonnet had more fruit than any head had a right to.

After lunch, there was meant to be a talk on music in Jane Austen's time but the speaker hadn't been able to attend because of the snow so it was decided that there'd be a showing of the 2005 film adaptation of *Pride and*

Prejudice instead and nobody complained. Well, nobody except Mrs Soames.

'I don't know what anybody sees in that version. That Mr Darcy is still wet behind the ears!' But she watched it all the same, harrumphing every time Matthew Macfadyen strode onto the screen only to be shushed by everybody else in the room.

Dame Pamela was too nervous to sit down and watch the film with everybody. She was pacing in her study, fretting over what Higgins had said to her. He'd planted a nasty little seed of doubt in her mind and now she was wringing her hands like a bad actress.

'But what does Higgins know?' she said to the empty study. He was one of the most cautious people she'd ever met and was one of the few people she'd ever been able to count on in her life for good, solid advice but what did she really know about him? He'd been in her employment for so long that she didn't know of any life outside of Purley Hall for Higgins. His parents had died a long time ago and he had a sister in a care home in Devon. He'd never married, never talked about relationships and only took two weeks holiday a year which was always spent in the same holiday cottage on the north Norfolk coast.

But, whatever Higgins's background, he had no business telling her what to do. Who was running this conference – him or her? He should stick to his own job, she told herself with an emphatic nod of the head. And, with her mind made up, she reached across her desk and picked up the item that had been causing so much trouble between them and placed it in her handbag.

CHAPTER 10

The great fireplace in the dining room had been lit and the orange flames licked over chunky logs, giving a homely feel to the grand room. Each table setting had the new white crockery edged with gold, bright silver cutlery, one crystal glass for water and a ruby-red one for wine. There was a cream linen napkin and an elegant cracker in emerald and gold and there were candles everywhere – snow-white and slim in silver candelabra and great fat red ones were lined along the fireplace.

Sparkling glass platters were piled high with oranges studded with cloves which scented the warm air, and there were pomegranates, grapes and pears, heaped and polished.

'Are we meant to eat those?' Mia asked Sarah.

'I wouldn't dare,' Sarah said, envisaging an avalanche of fruit if one so much as poked a grape.

'What's it going to look like on Christmas Day itself?' Mia said.

'Well, we don't have long to find out,' Sarah said.

Mia smiled. 'I still feel so awful leaving Will and Gabe to come here.'

'And Lloyd,' Sarah said.

'But I guess they've got to get used to life with a Janeite,' Mia said. 'We do need these little treats every now and then.'

On the other side of the room, Cassie lay in an old-fashioned pram which her doting Aunt Pamela had bought her, and Robyn and Dan sat either side of her.

'I will never get over how beautiful Purley is,' Robyn said to Dan. 'Do you ever get used to it?'

He shook his head. 'It's something you never take for granted,' he said. 'It's like a daily gift.'

Robyn nodded. 'I don't ever want to leave.'

'You don't have to,' he said and they smiled at each other as if they'd already been given the best Christmas present in the world.

Benedict, who was sitting beside Robyn, looked at the pair of them and chuckled. Young love, he thought, remembering the time he'd leapt into marriage and leapt straight back out almost as quickly.

After dinner, a hush descended as Dame Pamela stood up at the head of the table. She was wearing a dress in royal blue and had a pair of sapphire and diamond earrings dangling from her ears, the stones as large as birds' eggs.

'And now, I have something I've been dying to share with you,' she announced. 'It's a little Christmas present I bought for myself and I couldn't wait a moment longer before telling you about it. You might have read about it in the news. It came up for auction in September although the buyer wasn't named in the press.'

Everybody started whispering madly around the table. What could it be? It couldn't possibly be what they thought it was. Or could it? They waited in hushed anticipation as Higgins handed Dame Pamela a gift wrapped in bright gold paper with a thick crimson ribbon tied around it. Dame Pamela slowly untied the ribbon and unwrapped the hidden gift.

'It's book-shaped,' Rose whispered from the end of the table. 'I know a book at fifty paces.'

The guests leaned forward, necks craning to get their first glimpse of whatever Dame Pamela had bought at auction. Jackson Moore's eyes were out on stalks and Sarah was drumming her fingers on the linen tablecloth in anticipation. *It couldn't be, could it?* That's what everyone was thinking.

Sure enough, as the final fold of gold paper fell away to reveal a protective layer of fine tissue paper, they saw a book – or rather three books - but they weren't just any books – they looked old. About two hundred years old.

'It's the first edition!' Roberta screamed and everybody gasped, instantly knowing she was right. It would have been a very poor Jane Austen fan who hadn't heard of the auction at Sotheby's in September where a rare first edition of *Pride and Prejudice* had been sold to an anonymous bidder for a little under one hundred and eighty thousand pounds. And here it was, in this very room, in front of them, breathing the same air as them. Elizabeth Bennet and Mr Darcy – *the first edition*. The first book that had been sent out into the world to find its audience.

To look at it, you'd never know how very precious it was. It comprised of three slim volumes in dull brown boards with signs of water damage, and the spines were rough and had obviously seen some repairs. If it had been in a box at a car boot sale, most people wouldn't have looked twice at it but this book had journeyed from 1813 to be with them today and it was a most welcome guest.

'It's probably not a good idea to pass it around at the dining table but there will be an opportunity for you all to get a closer look at it later,' Dame Pamela promised as she wrapped up the three editions once more.

'How extraordinary!' Doris Norris said.

'I can't believe it!' Katherine said.

'Truly *wonderful!*' Gemma enthused.

Dame Pamela left the room with the books and coffee was served.

'I can't believe she bought that first edition,' Katherine said.

'Why not when you're as rich as Dame Pamela?' Warwick said. 'It's too good an opportunity to miss.'

'But think of the insurance!' Katherine said.

'Higgins has more than likely dealt with all the boring bits,' Warwick said. 'Dame Pamela's probably got nothing more pressing to think about other than cherishing it.'

'I can't imagine owning something like that,' Katherine said.

Warwick's dark eyebrows rose a fraction. 'But you already do.'

'What do you mean?'

'How many first edition Lorna Warwick's do you own?'

'Oh, Warwick! That's not the same thing at all!' Kay said.

He gave her a look of mock shock. 'It might be – *one* day. Who's to say which writers will be revered in two hundred years' time. My books might become very valuable.'

Katherine laughed but then she took his hand in hers. 'I'm sure they will be because you write wonderful stories.'

He smiled and took a sip of wine. Katherine watched as he drank and then her mind drifted back to the suitcase and his restless searching of the night before. As much as she loved him, she couldn't help thinking that he was up to something.

There was a showing of *Northanger Abbey* that evening and a lively discussion ensued about the sexiness of JJ Feild as Henry Tilney. Was it true to Austen or had Andrew Davies been at it again with his naughty pen?

'I think Henry Tilney is the sexiest of Austen's heroes,' Doris Norris said.

'What about Mr Darcy?' Rose asked.

'Well, he has that reserved sort of attractiveness,' Doris said. 'It's sexy but not overtly sexy, if you know what I mean.'

'I think Henry Tilney should definitely have a twinkle in his eye,' Mia said. 'Remember when he's dancing with Catherine and teasing her mercilessly? I've always imagined a naughty little smile in that scene.'

Discussion moved on - as it always did - to other Austen heroes.

'Jeremy Northam has always been my favourite Mr Knightley and he would've made a wonderful Tilney. His tone is just right,' Roberta said. 'He is serious yet subtle. Absolutely perfect.'

'Having seen Jonny Lee Miller again last night, I rather prefer him,' Doris Norris said.

'Oh, he wasn't right at all,' Mrs Soames said, her cheeks flaming in annoyance. 'Too soft. Not enough of a match for Emma. Besides, he was blond.'

'What's that got to do with anything?' Mia asked.

'I don't think blond suits an Austen hero. Except Mr Bingley,' Mrs Soames said.

'So you didn't like Rupert Penry-Jones as Captain Wentworth?' Mia said.

'Captain Wentworth should *not* be blond,' Mrs Soames asserted.

'Why not? His hair might have been bleached blond by the exposure to the sun on his ship,' Mia said.

'But blond is so – well – feminine,' Mrs Soames said.

Doris Norris gave a little chuckle. 'I once went out with a blond man and there was nothing feminine about him, let me assure you,' she said with a twinkle that was worthy of Henry Tilney himself.

'Now I come to think of it, there aren't that many blond heroes at all, are there?' Katherine said, enjoying the conversation immensely. It was just the sort of conversation she wouldn't be able to condone at Oxford.

Everybody looked thoughtful for a moment.

'There's Daniel Craig,' Rose suggested.

'Hmmm,' Roberta pondered. 'I'm not at all convinced about a blond Bond.'

'Colin Farrell went blond in *Alexander*,' Gemma said.

'And there was Dan Stevens in *Sense and Sensibility*,' Katherine said.

'But he was more feminine again - if you know what I mean,' Roberta said.

'Apart from that wood chopping scene,' Mia said with a little giggle.

'Julian Sands was very blond in *A Room with a View*,' Katherine said.

'And all of the Scarlet Pimpernels have been blond too,' Warwick said, pulling up a chair to join in. 'And Sean Bean as Sharpe.'

'Okay! Enough heroes already!' Sarah said.

'Oh, you can never have enough heroes!' Doris Norris said with a smile as she took another sip of sherry.

'I'd like to see Richard Armitage as Mr Darcy,' Kay said. 'I really do think that he's the forgotten Darcy.'

'What about Henry Cavill?' Mia said.

'As Darcy? Oh, no! He's far better suited to play Wickham,' Kay said.

And the conversation went on.

'I wonder what the next adaptation will be,' Rose said. 'I'm still waiting for a really good *Mansfield Park*. I don't think anyone's quite nailed it yet.'

'But does it really matter if it's good or not?' Mia said.

'What do you mean?' Rose asked.

'I mean, it doesn't matter how bad an adaptation is. It's still Jane Austen and that means it's a hundred times better than anything else that's on the television that evening.'

Rose nodded. 'You're right. A bad Jane Austen adaptation still beats anything else by a mile.'

'Yes but that *Lost in Austen* was just preposterous!' Mrs Soames said. 'Falling into the plot of *Pride and Prejudice*! It's ridiculous! Surely it would have been more realistic to have her finding a portal back to Regency times.'

'Yes but that's been done by so many books already,' Roberta said. 'I read two of them last week alone.'

'Anyway,' Kay said, 'haven't we *all* wanted to find ourselves in the midst of the Bennet family and meet Mr Darcy?'

'But for that – that – *heroine* to end up with Mr Darcy!' Mrs Soames said.

'So, you stayed with it until the end, then?' Kay teased.

Mrs Soames looked a little embarrassed. 'Well, there was nothing else on.'

'I think it was absolutely wonderful,' Doris Norris said. 'And just what so many of us have dreamed of for ourselves – a happy ending with Mr Darcy.'

CHAPTER 11

Dame Pamela was the first up on Christmas Day. It was still dark and she turned her bedside lamp on. Warm light filled the room as she placed her feet in her sequinned slippers. She didn't feel good. Her heart was racing and she'd had the most terrible nightmare that the Christmas tree had crashed down in the hallway, trapping several guests under an avalanche of baubles.

She yawned and got washed and dressed, blow-drying her hair and applying her make-up.

'How did my face become so *old*?' she asked the reflection that stared at her from out of the dressing table mirror. Beside the perfume bottles sat a silver-framed photograph of Dame Pamela in her much-loved production of *Sense and Sensibility*. She'd played Marianne Dashwood and had captured the hearts of every red-blooded man in the country. She picked up the photograph and stared at it, noting the flawless skin and the red-gold ringlets before returning her gaze to the ghostly face in the mirror once more. There was only one thing for it – *more* make-up.

Twenty minutes later, she was fully made-up and dressed, choosing the rich burgundy velvet gown trimmed with black lace. A pair of ruby stud earrings and her favourite ruby ring were chosen. Perfect for Christmas Day.

Leaving her bedroom, she walked the length of hallway that led to her study. It was lined with photographs of the great and the good and Dame Pamela nodded to a few of the friendly faces from the world of film and theatre including Sir Laurence Olivier who had once flirted with her at a charity dinner.

She loved her study first thing in the morning, opening the shutters and letting the first light in. It was a quiet time for her to contemplate the day that lay before her and to browse through some of the fan mail. People really were very sweet. She was still getting fan mail for films she'd made decades ago. Christmas cards too. Robyn had made a couple of cardboard Christmas trees painted in jolly colours to hold some of them and Dame Pamela smiled at them now. She adored her fans as much as they adored her and that had been one of the reasons she'd bought the first edition of *Pride and Prejudice* – because she didn't think of it as buying it for herself but rather for all her fellow Austen fans.

The conference was going so well, she thought. She would hold the memory of her guests' faces when she'd brought out the first edition of *Pride and Prejudice* for many years to come. It had been a wonderful, bonding moment between her and the other Janeites and she couldn't resist opening the safe which was hidden behind a painting of herself in the role of Ophelia in *Hamlet*. Higgins had told her that it wasn't a very original place to have a safe but Dame Pamela had adored the idea of having it behind her portrait and wouldn't listen to any advice. But, that morning, when she removed the painting and entered the code, her heart almost stopped because the first edition was no longer there.

Mia couldn't help it. She was worse than a child on Christmas morning and was out of bed way before the first streaks of light brightened the land.

'Sarah!' she whispered in her sister's ear. 'Sarah – it's Christmas!'

'What?' Sarah muttered something from under her duvet and turned over.

Mia tried again. 'We'll be late!' she said.

Sarah was sitting upright in a flash. 'Late? Didn't my alarm go off?'

Mia grinned.

'It hasn't gone off yet, has it, Mia?'

'Not exactly,' she said.

'Oh, Mia!'

'But it's Christmas morning and you shouldn't spend it *sleeping!*' she chided.

'It doesn't look like I'm going to get much choice in the matter, does it?' Sarah swung her legs out of bed and carefully put her slippers on – left then right.

'Presents!' Mia shouted.

'Not yet,' Sarah said. 'Wash and dress first!'

Mia sighed but then washed and dressed in record time but then had to wait for Sarah who took simply ages to do everything perfectly and in the right order.

Finally, they were ready.

'Open yours first!' Mia said, handing her sister a tiny package wrapped in metallic green paper.

Sarah took the package and opened it neatly, prising the tape from both ends of the package without ripping the paper at all and then unfolding it to reveal a box. She put the paper to one side and placed the box in the palm of her hand, looking at it for a maddeningly long time.

'Open it!' Mia urged from her home on the carpet where she was sitting cross-legged as if in some yoga position.

Sarah did and then gasped at the contents. It was a cameo brooch depicting a lovely lady with long flowing hair.

'Oh, Mia! It's beautiful. Wherever did you find it?'

Mia grinned. 'At a tabletop sale in a little village in the Cotswolds. Gabe took us out for the day and we pottered around and found all sorts of amazing places but, when I saw this, I just knew you'd love it!'

'I do! It's gorgeous.'

'Put it on!'

Sarah, who was wearing an immaculate cashmere jumper, swallowed hard and Mia immediately knew what she was thinking and leapt up from the floor, opening one of the drawers in which Sarah had folded and placed some of her clothes.

'Here we are,' she said a second later, flying back across the room with a chiffon scarf that matched the colour of Sarah's jumper. 'So you don't put a hole in your jumper.'

Sarah smiled up at Mia as she placed the scarf around her neck before pinning the brooch to it. They knew each other's little quirks so well.

'Would you like your present now or later?' Sarah teased.

Mia laughed. 'What do you think?'

Sarah laughed too and went to get her handbag. Mia cocked her head to one side. Experience had told her that the best presents were often the smallest and, if it fitted in Sarah's handbag, then it was bound to be a good one.

'Merry Christmas, Mia,' Sarah said, handing over a flat gold package a moment later.

Mia held it in her hands for a moment, trying to get the measure of it. It was light and almost completely flat like an envelope.

'Come on then – open it! You dragged me out of bed at the crack of dawn for that!'

Mia took a deep breath and ripped the paper. Whereas Sarah's gift had been opened with meticulous care, Mia tore through hers like a naughty puppy. She'd been right, it was an envelope. She bit her lip and then opened it. It was a letter confirming the booking of a holiday cottage on the Devon coast. But not just any holiday cottage. It was the grand country manor house that had been used in the 1995 film adaptation of *Sense and Sensibility*. Barton Cottage – the home of the Dashwood sisters.

'Sarah!' Mia cried.

Sarah grinned. 'You didn't guess, then?'

'No! I thought it might be theatre tickets or a book token or something. Never this!'

'I checked the dates with Gabe,' Sarah said, 'and it doesn't clash with school terms or anything.'

'You always think of everything,' Mia said.

'Of course,' Sarah said with a smile and then she looked serious for a moment. 'I wasn't sure if you'd want to go again what with all the memories of Alec,' she added, thinking of the man they'd met on their last holiday there – the man who had torn them apart for three long years.

'No – I mean – yes, I do! It's the most beautiful place in the world and I won't let Alec take that away from me.'

'Good,' Sarah said. 'I'd hoped that was how you'd feel about it.'

'Oh, I can't wait for Gabe to see it! He's going to love it. And Will's going to adore the garden and the beach.'

Sarah nodded. 'You'll have a brilliant time.'

'And you'll come too, won't you, Sarah? You and Lloyd?'

'No, no – this is for you and Gabe and Will.'

'Oh, but you *must* come!' Mia cried. 'There's so much room and it'll be so much fun.'

Sarah smiled. 'Well, maybe for just a couple of nights.'

When Katherine walked out of the en suite, her hair still wet from her shower, she saw the most peculiar sight – Warwick's rump was high in the air and the contents of his suitcase was strewn around the floor. He was at it again and, this time, she was going to confront him.

'What *are* you doing?' she cried.

Warwick span around, a defeated look on his face. 'I – erm,' he began, a strange, sickly smile on his face. 'I think I've forgotten your Christmas present.'

'Oh, Warwick! I told you not to worry,' she said, relief filling her that that was all he'd been hiding from her.

'What? Are you kidding?' he said, his dark eyes widening.

'No,' Katherine said, walking over to the dressing table and combing her hair. 'I'm not like other women – you don't have to butter me up with presents all the time.'

'But it's Christmas!' Warwick said.

'Christmas is a modern convention which simply exists to make money.'

'Oh, you don't believe that for one minute,' Warwick said. 'Besides, every woman who says she doesn't want flowers or chocolates or any sort of gifts is just testing you.'

Katherine turned around from the mirror and gave him a wry smile. 'I'm not testing you, Warwick. The fact that I've got you a present and you haven't got me one doesn't bother me at all.'

'But I *have* got you one!' Warwick protested. 'I was sure I'd brought it too but I – well – never mind. I'm obviously not as well organised as you are.'

'I know,' Katherine said matter-of-factly as she walked over to her own suitcase and unzipped the compartment on the top. She brought out a present that was wrapped in green and gold striped paper: neat and classic – so like Katherine, Warwick couldn't help thinking. It was book-shaped but Warwick didn't like to try and guess presents. He liked to be surprised.

'Merry Christmas,' she said, kissing him on the cheek and handing him his gift.

Warwick grinned as he tore the paper. It was a book but he wasn't prepared for which book it was.

'Now, don't get excited – it's not a first edition of *Pride and Prejudice*,' Katherine warned him.

'Oh, my god!' he said a moment later, sliding the book out of the paper. 'It's better than that,' he said with a long, low whistle. It was a first edition of one of his own early books. Warwick had mentioned how he'd absent-mindedly posted copies to friends and fans and had discovered that he hadn't kept a single copy for himself. It had been a small print run too and it was notoriously difficult to get hold of now.

'Where did you find it?' he asked, his mouth hanging open.

'I have my sources,' Katherine said.

Warwick shook his head. 'You're a miracle worker,' he said.

'Now, don't you feel bad because you didn't get me a present?'

'But I *did!*' he cried.

She laughed at his distraught face.

'I really did,' he said, 'and you'll have it as soon as we're back at the vicarage.'

For a few moments, Dame Pamela found that she couldn't move. She was literally petrified. Think, she kept telling herself. *Think!* Had she really put the first edition back in the safe as Higgins had expressly told her to do straight after dinner or had she placed it on her desk or left it somewhere else?

She tried to retrace her steps after dinner but she could only remember it being a jumble of broken conversations with her guests. Had she come straight to her study afterwards or had she absent-mindedly placed the book down somewhere else? Dear, oh dear! Why was her memory so bad these day? Why couldn't she *remember?*

CHAPTER 12

Kay Ashton gazed out of one of the library windows, her eyes taking in the beauty of it all. She'd just spent a rather uncomfortable ten minutes talking to Jackson Moore and was trying to work out what exactly he was doing at the conference. She'd managed to slip away from him when Higgins had come in a moment ago to top up the little bowls of mint humbugs on the tables and she sincerely hoped that the strange man wouldn't catch her eye again.

'Hello,' Adam said as he came into the room.

'Oh, Adam!' Kay said, relieved to see him.

'You okay?' he asked.

Kay pulled a face. 'It's that Jackson Moore,' she whispered.

Adam looked in the direction she was nodding in. 'What about him?' he whispered back.

'He just doesn't seem to fit in here,' Kay said. 'He's been prowling around the library taking books down and examining them since I came in and he does this nervous throat-clearing thing. It's very unnerving!'

'I know what you mean,' Adam said. 'Gemma and I tried to talk to him yesterday and we couldn't get a thing out of him.'

'I've just tried talking to him too,' Kay said, 'and he just doesn't seem-' she paused, searching for the right word, '*real.*'

They turned to look at Jackson Moore. He was still pulling books out from the shelves and examining them carefully.

'He's probably just one of those blokes who gets on better with books than with people,' Adam said.

'You mean like you were before you met me?' Kay said.

'Exactly,' Adam said with a grin.

Dame Pamela was pacing up and down in her study, twisting one of her diamond rings round and round her finger.

'Did you come straight back to the study, madam?' Higgins asked.

'That's what I've been trying to remember,' Dame Pamela said, 'only it's not that easy to remember the order of things these days. I was talking to everyone, you see.'

Higgins nodded. 'Can you remember if you were holding *Pride and Prejudice* when you were talking to everyone? Maybe you let somebody hold it?'

'Yes, of course I did. I promised everyone they could have a look at it but I was keeping an eye on it.'

'We'll have to check everybody,' Higgins said. 'Do room searches and look through luggage.'

'Oh, must we? It's Christmas Day.'

'And your first edition of *Pride and Prejudice* is missing,' Higgins pointed out.

'But I don't want to cause panic. Not today,' Dame Pamela said, giving her ring its biggest twist yet.

'What would you like to do, madam?' Higgins asked, his face more serious than Dame Pamela had ever seen it before.

'Why don't we just leave things for a bit and see if it turns up?'

Higgins didn't look happy. 'Madam-'

'Nobody's going to leave, are they? Just look at the snow out there. It's not as if somebody has stolen it and is about to make off with it.'

Dame Pamela walked over to the window and looked out over the snow-covered garden. She didn't speak for a moment but then she turned to look back at Higgins.

'And I think I'd like to speak to Benedict,' she said.

Benedict Harcourt was sitting in the Yellow Drawing Room enjoying a cigar he'd found in the drawer of a rather fine Georgian bureau. He didn't normally smoke cigars –

he couldn't afford to - but it was Christmas and his sister surely wouldn't begrudge him a cigar or two, would she?

He looked around the room, marvelling at the paintings and wondering how much they'd cost. That landscape, for example. It looked like it could have been painted by some long-dead painter like Constable and was probably worth a penny or two. He could probably pay his mortgage off with what it would fetch and set up that company he'd been planning.

He sighed. That was the trouble with money. You needed money in order to get money and, well, he didn't have any money. It did seem a tad unfair to him that some people seemed to attract money whilst others never got anywhere near it. Take his sister. What did she get paid for her last film? He shuddered to think. And the cost and upkeep of Purley Hall was enough to make your eyes water. She was one lucky dame, that was for sure, whilst he was a great big loser with nothing in his pockets but a stick of gum and a two-inch tear.

'Ah, there you are, Benedict,' Dame Pamela said as she entered the room in a flurry of burgundy.

'Pamsy!' he said, springing out of the armchair and puffing a plume of smoke into her face. 'Merry Christmas, darling sister!'

'Yes, yes. Merry Christmas to you too,' she said, accepting his kiss none too graciously. 'Sit down, Benedict,' she said, taking a seat on the sofa opposite him.

'You seem a little flustered,' he said.

Dame Pamela nodded, twisting the great diamond ring once again. Benedict's eyes were almost out on stalks as he noticed it. 'What exactly are you doing here, Benedict?' she asked him a moment later.

'What do you mean?' he asked. 'I've told you, I came to see you, Pamsy!'

Dame Pamela glared at him, her expression echoing her role as Lady Catherine de Bough and he instantly knew that she didn't believe him.

'We don't see you from one year to the next and then we only get the occasional phone call when you're in financial difficulties.'

'Well, I'm sorry if you think I'm a bad brother.'

'I didn't say that. It's just the way you are and we're used to it but it makes me wonder what you're doing here now,' she said.

Benedict took a deep breath. 'What's this all about?' he asked.

'You tell me.'

'You're the one who's anxious,' he pointed out.

Dame Pamela sighed. 'You're right. I am. Something's gone missing. Something very precious.'

'What?'

'The first edition.'

Benedict stubbed out the fat cigar in a little porcelain dish on a mahogany side table, making Dame Pamela wince. 'It's missing?'

'Yes.'

'And what's that got to do with me being here?'

Dame Pamela blinked but didn't say anything.

Benedict nodded slowly. 'I see,' he said at last. 'You think I've got it, don't you? You think I've come here like some petty thief to take whatever I could get my hands on. Is that it?'

'No,' Dame Pamela said but her voice didn't seem to back her up.

'You really think I'd do something like that? Just come here and steal from you?'

'Benedict, I don't think that at all but-'

'Because that's all I am to you, isn't it? I'm the brother who's just after a handout.' He stood up and marched towards the door and, before Dame Pamela could stop him, he'd stormed out, slamming the great door behind him.

Dan was doing his best to straighten the drunken angel on the top of the Christmas tree yet again as Dame Pamela left the Yellow Drawing Room.

'She's been at the whiskey again,' Dan said as he saw his sister.

'I could do with a glass myself,' Dame Pamela said.

Dan came back down to earth from the ladder. 'What's wrong?'

Dame Pamela shook her head and Dan could see tears swimming in her bright eyes. 'I can't find the first edition,' she said.

Dan's mouth dropped open. '*Pride and Prejudice*?'

Dame Pamela nodded.

'How long's it been missing?'

'I couldn't find it this morning,' she said.

'But you put it back in the safe last night?'

'That's just it – I really can't remember but I've looked absolutely everywhere and I'm at my wits' end!'

'Calm down,' Dan said, placing his hands on his sister's shoulders. 'Now, if you've looked everywhere and Higgins has looked everywhere-'

'He has.'

'Then we need to make an announcement.'

'But it's Christmas Day!' Dame Pamela protested.

'Yes, and somebody might have gone off with one hell of a Christmas present,' Dan said. 'Merry Christmas by the way,' he added.

'Yes, Merry Christmas,' Dame Pamela said absent-mindedly.

'I think we should make an announcement as soon as possible,' Dan continued. 'Look, we've got that talk about Jane Austen's use of dialogue starting in twenty minutes. Why don't you do it then?'

Dame Pamela looked to her left and then looked to her right as if trying to find an excuse or an exit out of the awful situation she now found herself in.

'But what if I've just misplaced it somewhere?' she asked.

'But what if you haven't? What if somebody else has picked it up – by accident even – and doesn't even realise what they've done? Or maybe somebody's seen it. It might all be resolved in no time and you'll be able to relax again.'

Dame Pamela nodded. 'All right,' she said. 'I'll make a brief announcement.'

'Good,' Dan said, 'and I'll have a good hunt around in the meantime. Maybe Benedict could help.'

'Oh, that's another thing,' Dame Pamela said.

'What?'

'We had a little misunderstanding,' Dame Pamela said.

'What kind of misunderstanding?'

Dame Pamela began with the ring twisting again. 'I might have accused him of taking the first edition.'

'Oh, Pammy!'

'Don't scold me! I feel dreadful enough as it is!'

'But you don't really think he's taken it, do you?'

Dame Pamela sighed. 'I don't know what to think,' she said.

'Right, well, you go and get ready for the announcement and I'll have a look for *Pride and Prejudice*. And Benedict. Okay?'

'Okay,' she said. 'Thank you, Dan. I don't know what I'd do without you.'

They both smiled at each other and left the hallway just as the angel on the Christmas tree nose dived towards a red bauble.

CHAPTER 13

Doris Norris was trying to relax. She'd been looking forward to the morning talk about Jane Austen's use of dialogue but her mind kept drifting back to the night before. It was silly really. She'd taken off her engagement ring because her fingers had swollen. But where had she put it? By the sink? On the dressing table? She really couldn't remember and she couldn't find it anywhere.

She looked down at the thin gold band of her wedding ring. She never took that off; it hadn't budged since the day Henry had placed it on her finger at their wedding and had kissed her so passionately that the feathers on her mother's hat had vibrated in alarm. The ring wouldn't actually come off now even if she wanted it to. It was a part of her and she would take it with her into the next world.

But where on earth was the engagement ring? It hadn't been an expensive ring but the garnets were much loved by her and she'd worn it every day since her husband had presented it to her on a day out in Brighton. They'd walked along the sea front eating ice cream, the salt wind in their hair, and he'd taken her hand in his and told her that he wasn't Mr Darcy but that he hoped he could make her happy anyway. He'd been hiding the ring in his jacket pocket which explained why he'd constantly been tapping it all day. Doris had guessed what he was up to but had managed to look surprised all the same and they'd celebrated with a fish supper before catching the last train home.

She'd lost her dear Henry eight years ago and now she'd lost his ring. She blinked the tears away as Dame Pamela entered the room. She'd try to put the ring out of her mind for now and look for it again later.

Dan had turned Dame Pamela's study upside down searching for *Pride and Prejudice* but it obviously wasn't there. He'd hunted through her bedroom and had looked in all of the public rooms too, scanning the shelves of books everywhere in case it had been put away by mistake but there was no sign of it. Of course there wasn't, he thought. He didn't want to scare his sister but he had a nasty feeling about this whole business. He'd been nervous the moment he'd seen it in the dining room, his sister proudly displaying it to a room full of relative strangers. She wouldn't have them called strangers, though. She'd told him umpteen times that the bond of Jane Austen turned fans into friends and friends into family but Dan didn't buy that. As far as he was concerned, somebody had stolen the first edition and he intended to find out who it was.

It was as he was climbing the stairs that he spotted Benedict. He was standing on the landing looking out on to the snowy landscape.

'Hello,' Dan said as he approached him.

'Oh, hello,' Benedict said, turning around. His face looked pale and the lines around his eyes looked deeper than usual.

'Pammy told me what happened,' Dan said, deciding to just come out with it and speed the healing process up a bit.

Benedict nodded as if he expected no less. 'I can't understand it, Danny boy,' he said, using his old nickname for his little brother. 'How can she think that of me?'

Dan put his hand on his brother's shoulder. 'Let's get a cup of tea.'

They walked down to the kitchen together. Higgins was bustling around arranging shortbread for after the first lecture of the morning and Benedict pinched a slice from one of the trays. They waited until Higgins had left and then Benedict sat down at the long pine table in front of the AGA.

'I'm sorry,' Dan said as he made them both a cup of tea. 'This hasn't been much of a homecoming for you, has it?'

Benedict swallowed the last of his shortbread. 'I guess I've brought this on myself,' he said. 'I know I've done my fair share of running to Pamsy for handouts over the years. I suppose it's only fair that she suspects me now when I turn up out of the blue.'

'It wasn't fair of her to accuse you like that. I guess she's just really worried about this book.'

Benedict took a sip of the tea that Dan handed him. 'What on earth's she doing buying such a thing? What did it cost her?'

'Well, I remember hearing something about the auction a few months back. I think it was the best part of two hundred thousand pounds.'

Benedict spluttered on his tea. 'Good grief! Two hundred thousand pounds – for a *book?*'

'A very special book,' Dan said as he sat down opposite him. 'Isn't it the nation's favourite novel? It's certainly the most loved of all of Jane Austen's and fans will pay a premium for something like that especially a first edition.'

'You could buy a house with that kind of money,' Benedict said.

'But Pammy has a house already.'

'Or start a business.'

Dan looked at him. 'You haven't taken it, have you?'

Benedict's eyes widened. 'What?

'Sorry,' Dan said, quickly shaking his head. 'It's just when you mentioned starting a business.'

Benedict glared at him. 'Look, I know I might have made a mess of things in the past but that's all going to change and I don't need to steal or take handouts from my sister in order to do it.'

Dan nodded and noticed that Benedict had turned quite red. 'Okay,' he said, 'enough about this first edition. So, tell me your plans for the future.'

Benedict cleared his throat and turned even redder and then reached out across the table to steal another piece of shortbread in an attempt to delay answering the question.

Dame Pamela walked to the front of the audience who were seated in the library for the morning lecture. She beamed a smile.

'Merry Christmas, everybody!' she said and everybody chimed the same wish back at her except Mrs Soames in the front room who was checking her watch in disapproval of Dame Pamela being two minutes late.

'I'd like to make a very short announcement before the talk this morning.' She took a deep breath. 'I seem to have misplaced the first edition of *Pride and Prejudice*.'

There was a gasp from the audience.

'And I'm hoping you can all keep a look out for it. I'm sure it will turn up sooner or later but it's very delicate and I'm conscious that it might get damaged.'

'It's been stolen!' somebody hissed from the middle of the room.

'Somebody's taken it!' another voice said.

'I'm sure it's nothing to worry about,' Dame Pamela said, her hands flapping in the air like anxious butterflies. 'It's just me being absent-minded.'

'You wouldn't get me being absent-minded with a book that's worth a fortune,' Mrs Soames muttered from the front row.

'Now, it's my very great pleasure to introduce Dr Katherine Roberts who is going to talk to us about dialogue in Jane Austen's work.'

There was a round of applause as Katherine stood up and made her way to the front of the room. Dame Pamela walked down the aisle between the rows of chairs towards the door. She normally stayed for all the talks but she couldn't settle with the book missing and so thought it better if she left.

'Pamela?' Robyn, who'd been sitting in the back row with Cassie sleeping in her arms, stood up. 'Is there anything I can do to help? Do you want me to have a good hunt around?'

Dame Pamela shook her head. 'Dan's already onto it and Higgins has spent hours searching everywhere too.'

They left the library together, Cassie in Robyn's arms. 'Oh, this is awful,' Robyn said. 'Do you think somebody's taken it?'

'I don't even want to consider that possibility yet,' Dame Pamela said. 'I mean, we're all friends here, aren't we?'

'I like to think so but maybe the temptation got too much for someone.'

'But we're such a small community. The risk of being caught is too great,' Dame Pamela said. 'Especially with us all being snowed in.'

'I don't think that would put anybody off,' Robyn said. 'Not somebody who was serious about it.'

'Don't you?' Dame Pamela said, her eyes wide with worry.

Robyn shook her head. 'If we can't find the first edition anywhere and nobody comes forward with it then perhaps we'd better think seriously about what we're going to do next.'

CHAPTER 14

Roberta was fidgeting and it wasn't because of the itchy tweed skirt she was wearing although that was enough reason to make anybody fidget. She was fidgeting because she was nervous and she couldn't concentrate any more on the talk.

'What is it?' Rose demanded of her sister, nudging her in the ribs with an angry elbow.

'Don't do that! You know I hate it!' Roberta whispered.

'Then stop fidgeting!'

Roberta sighed. Rose could be such a bully sometimes. Honestly, they were both in their seventies now but, sometimes, it was as if they were still children.

Roberta stood up abruptly and grabbed her sister's arm and marched her out of the library and into the hallway.

'What do you think you're doing? I wanted to stay and ask that nice Dr Roberts some questions,' Rose said.

'But this is important.'

Rose sighed. 'What have you done?' She'd learned over the years that, whenever her sister, Roberta said 'this is important', she'd done something wrong.

'It's about the first edition,' Roberta said.

'Of *Pride and Prejudice*?'

'No, the latest Warwick Lawton novel! Of *course* of *Pride and Prejudice*!'

'Sarcasm doesn't become you, Roberta,' Rose said.

Roberta sighed. 'I'm sorry but I'm really worried. I think I've done something terrible.'

'You'd better tell me what's going on right now,' Rose said, pushing her up the stairs. Once they'd arrived in their twin bedroom and closed the door, Roberta walked over to her bedside table and picked up three old books and brought them over for Rose to see.

'What are these?' Rose asked.

'I think it's the first edition.

Rose's face paled. 'You took it?'

'I found it in the library. Dame Pamela said we could borrow any of the books in there. I didn't think I was doing any harm.'

'Is it the first edition?' Rose said, taking one of the volumes from her sister.

'I don't know,' Roberta said. 'How do you tell these things?'

'I have no idea,' Rose said. 'I wasn't wearing my glasses when Dame Pamela held it up at dinner.'

'Neither was I but it certainly looks old.'

Rose opened the cover and looked inside. 'I can't see a date anywhere but it's quite badly damaged. Maybe the page with the date has been torn out. Are there dates in the other two volumes?'

Roberta sat on the edge of the bed and opened the other volumes. 'No. I can't see anything. This page is awfully damaged. Maybe the date was on here.'

'We've *got* to return it to Dame Pamela right away,' Rose said.

Roberta looked truly terrified. 'Oh, please don't make me!'

'Tell her you took it by mistake. She'll be so relieved to have it back that she won't care about anything else.'

'I'll be arrested!' Roberta shrieked. 'They'll put me in prison!'

'Nobody's going to put you in prison,' Rose said. 'Now, get a grip of yourself.'

'Can't I just put it back in the library? That *is* where I got it from.'

Rose looked thoughtful for a moment. There was some sense in what Roberta was saying and she didn't want to cause a fuss – not on Christmas Day. Maybe returning it to the library – quickly and quietly – was the best option.

'Okay,' Rose said. 'We'll return it to the library.'

'And then maybe we could alert somebody to it – pick it out from the shelves and ask if it's the first edition?' Roberta said.

'Let's just get it back to the library first,' Rose said.

But, as they walked downstairs with the three volumes hidden in a hessian bag, they saw that their plan wasn't going to work because there was a group of people in the library chatting to Dr Roberts after her talk.

Roberta turned to Rose, her face full of anguish. 'What do we do now?' she whispered.

'We come back later,' Rose said, pushing her sister back up the stairs with a bony finger.

There was even more excited chatter and noise than usual in the dining room of Purley Hall when one o'clock arrived because Christmas lunch was about to be served. Higgins, who was being aided by two helpers, made sure that everybody had everything they could wish for and there was wine, goose, pigs in blankets, roast vegetables and greens, thick gravy and home-made cranberry sauce and plates were piled high. The candles were all lit and the fire roared in the hearth.

Rose and Roberta tried not to think about the first edition hidden under one of the beds in their room, Benedict tried to forget that his sister had accused him of robbing her and Dan tried not to cast quizzical looks around the table, trying to wheedle out a possible traitor amongst the Janeites.

After lunch, the main lights of the dining room were dimmed and Higgins entered with a great silver tray on which sat the biggest Christmas pudding the guests had ever seen, its blue flames licking happily around it.

Then came the crackers and the room filled with the sound of little bangs and laughter as terrible jokes were read out and jolly paper hats were placed on heads but the real surprise was the trinkets inside the crackers. Gasps were heard around the room as the guests discovered silver charm bracelets, fountain pens and diamante pendants.

'Where on earth did you buy these crackers, Dame Pamela?' Mia asked from the other side of the table.

'They're the best I've ever seen!' she said, putting on the silver charm bracelet.

Dame Pamela beamed with pride. 'Well, I couldn't find exactly what I wanted in the shops so I had Higgins dismantle them all and put in individual gifts I chose myself.'

There was a round of applause and an embarrassed Higgins took a little bow.

It was then that Warwick stood up and cleared his throat.

'On behalf of everybody here, I would like to thank our extraordinary hostess, Dame Pamela, for this wonderful meal and yet another fantastic conference. You know *exactly* how to make people feel welcome and you know that everybody likes to be spoilt once in a while. To Dame Pamela!'

Everybody raised their glasses.

'To Dame Pamela!' they chorused.

Dame Pamela's hands fluttered in front of her face as if she was batting away their attention but everybody could see that she was revelling in it.

No activities had been planned for Christmas Day afternoon although there was the promise of dancing in the evening to look forward to. Meanwhile, some of the guests chose to watch the Queen's speech on the television in the Yellow Drawing Room whilst others were sprawled in various armchairs, sofas and beds, feeling wonderfully replete after having eaten a lot of very good food.

Kay and Adam were sitting in the library and Kay was watching Higgins as he moved around the room, making sure everyone had enough tea and coffee.

'You know who would make a really cute couple?' Kay whispered to Adam.

'Who?'

'Higgins and Doris Norris,' Kay declared with a huge smile.

'Are you joking?' Adam asked.

'No. Why would I be joking about such a serious business as love?'

'Kay – I thought you promised you weren't going to match-make anymore. I distinctly remember you saying-'

'Yes but they'd be so *perfect* together, don't you think?'

'No, I don't!' Adam said, his eyes wide with horror. 'That's the worst match you've come up with yet.'

'Why?' Kay said, looking wounded.

'Well,' Adam said, stroking his chin, 'Doris just isn't Higgins's type.'

'No? Well, who is?'

'I don't think any woman is his type.'

Kay looked confused for a moment and then clarity descended. 'Oh!' she said. 'How do you know?'

'Just an inkling,' Adam said. 'I walked by his room last night and his door was ajar and I heard him singing.'

'What was he singing?'

'The soundtrack to *Yentl*,' Adam said.

'But that doesn't *mean* anything,' Kay said with an exasperated sigh.

'It does when you're singing it to a poster of Mandy Patinkin.'

Mia was still admiring her silver charm bracelet. It was such a thoughtful gift. The charms included miniature books, a dear little bonnet, a bouquet of flowers and a heart. She was going to find herself a quiet corner somewhere in Purley Hall so she could sit and admire it and also ring Gabe and speak to her darling little boy, William, and see how their Christmas Day was going. She was missing them so much but she knew that they'd be having a fabulous time with neighbours, Shelley and Pie and Bingley the dog.

Opening a door into one of the rooms at the back of Purley Hall, Mia froze. There was a man bending double and it didn't take long for Mia to recognise Jackson Moore and he was going through a lady's handbag.

'Excuse me!' Mia cried, consternation in her voice.

He span around, obviously surprised.

'What are you doing?' she asked, a frown on her face.

'I was just-' he stopped as a voice from a winged chair by the window interrupted him.

'He was just getting my pills,' Doris Norris said.

Mia narrowed her eyes as Jackson Moore rooted in Doris's handbag once again, bringing out a small packet of tablets which he took over to her.

'How kind you are,' she told him. 'You two have met, haven't you?'

Mia's face softened a little as she joined them by the window and Jackson gave her a tight smile. 'Yes,' she said. 'Are you all right, Doris? Can I get you anything?'

'No, thank you, my dear. This kind man brought me a glass of water and I have my tablets now.'

Mia sat on a chair next to her. 'It's been an exciting day, hasn't it?'

'Oh, yes!' Doris said. 'I was going to have a rest in my room but I didn't feel like the climb upstairs.'

'I can help you,' Jackson Moore said.

Doris shook her head. 'That's so kind of you but I think I'll just close my eyes here for a little while.'

Mia watched as Doris shut her eyes. Jackson Moore walked over to the door and picked up Doris's handbag and brought it over to her.

'Can I get *you* anything, Mia?' he asked, stroking his dense moustache.

She shook her head, disliking the sound of her name on his tongue. 'No, thank you,' she said.

'You know, you look just like my daughter,' he told her.

Mia winced. 'Really?' she said.

He nodded thoughtfully. 'She has *exactly* the same sulky look as you do.'

Mia's mouth dropped open at his rudeness and she watched as he left the room. 'Well, I-' she paused as Doris opened an eye.

'Isn't he a character?' she giggled.

'Yes!' Mia said. 'The sort of character that any author would make sure gets his comeuppance!'

CHAPTER 15

Mia didn't usually take an afternoon nap but there was something about sitting in that quiet room with Doris that made her nod off and, when she awoke, Doris was gone.

She got up and stretched and that's when she became aware of the raised voices - voices that were filled with anxiety.

'She just fell!' somebody shouted.

'She's so pale. Someone call an ambulance!'

'She's had a heart attack!'

Mia opened the door into the hallway and saw the crowd at the bottom of the stairs. She pushed her way through and let out a cry as she saw the body on the floor. It was Doris Norris and her eyes were closed and her face deadly white.

Panic ensued as people talked over each other.

'We need to call an ambulance.'

'It'll never get through.'

'Is there a first aider?'

'It's too late for that – just look at her!'

'Don't say that. Call an ambulance!'

Dan was already on the phone.

'Sarah!' Mia was shouting. 'Sarah does first aid.'

Sarah was already on the landing having heard the commotion from upstairs and was by Doris's side in an instant. It often surprised people that Sarah did first aid. Her OCD usually meant that she kept people she didn't know at a safe distance from her but she'd once signed up for a class called 'Cure Your OCD' and one of the tasks had been to learn first aid. Well, Sarah's OCD hadn't been cured but she'd never forgotten the first aid.

'She's not breathing,' Sarah said, looking up from the floor.

'Oh, my god!' Mia shrieked.

'Doris!' Dame Pamela cried.

There followed an anxious few moments as Sarah administered first aid, giving chest compressions followed by rescue breaths.

'They're sending the air ambulance,' Dan said a moment later. 'We're to clear a space – out in the back garden will be best – and a route into the house for the stretcher.'

Warwick stepped forward. 'That's something I can help with.'

'Count me in,' Adam said, stepping forward.

'Me too,' Benedict said.

'And me!' Katherine said. She'd always kept her own cottage pathway clear of snow even in the deepest of Oxfordshire winters.

'Good,' Dan said. 'Higgins – we're going to need shovels and spades.'

'Right away, sir,' Higgins said.

'How's she doing?' Dan asked.

Sarah looked up from the carpet. 'She's breathing.'

'Oh, thank god!' Dame Pamela said.

Dan, Benedict, Adam, Katherine and Warwick donned coats, hats, scarves and gloves and left the house.

'Doris?' Sarah said. 'Can you hear me? An ambulance is on its way. Hang on in there. We're all here with you.'

'Fetch a blanket,' Gemma said. 'You've got to keep her warm.'

Mia stepped forward and squeezed Sarah's shoulder. 'You were amazing,' she said.

'I only wish I could do more,' Sarah said.

'I was just talking to her,' Mia said, tears in her eyes. 'She looked tired but I had no idea that this was going to happen.'

'Of course you didn't. Nobody can predict something like this,' Sarah said.

'I fell asleep,' Mia said. 'I was asleep when she was suffering like this.'

'Don't blame yourself,' Sarah said.

'I'm going outside to help,' Mia said.

Sarah nodded. 'Well, wrap up warm first, okay?'

Mia ran upstairs for her coat, boots and hat before joining the snow-clearing party in the garden. Higgins had found a motley collection of shovels and spades in varying degrees of decrepitude but they did the job and a large square was soon clear of snow and work began on a pathway back to the house and the patio doors that opened out from the Yellow Drawing Room.

They only just made it in time when the helicopter arrived. Everybody inside rushed towards the back of the house to look out of the window as the huge yellow helicopter landed and two men leapt out with a stretcher.

Sarah and Dame Pamela were with Doris when they arrived. They briefed them on what they thought had happened, watching as the men carefully attended to their patient, placing her on the stretcher. Sarah straightened the ambulance blanket and handed one of the men Doris's handbag and a little bag of clothes and toiletries which Rose had gathered together from Doris's bedroom.

'She's got medication in there,' Sarah told them and they nodded. 'Shall I come too?'

'We won't be able to promise you a ride back,' one of the men said.

'It's all right, Sarah,' Dame Pamela said, laying a hand on her arm. 'We'll keep close contact with the hospital from here.'

They followed the men through the hall and into the Yellow Drawing Room, stopping at the patio doors as they took Doris towards the waiting helicopter.

The guests who'd been shovelling the snow were still outside and watched as the helicopter slowly took off, its bright bulk soon becoming nothing more than a little dot in the snow-heavy sky.

CHAPTER 16

'Poor Doris,' Robyn said to Dan as he came back into the warmth and took his coat off.

'She didn't look good,' Dan said, 'but she's in the best hands now. Where's Cassie?'

'Higgins took her to the kitchen. She got scared with all the noise.'

'And how's Pammy coping?'

Robyn didn't have time to answer Dan's question because there was a sudden cry.

'My handbag!' Mrs Soames cried. 'Somebody's taken my handbag. I left it right here on this chair.'

'Are you sure it was there?' Rose asked.

'Of *course* I'm sure!' Mrs Soames said, her bosom rising in annoyance at being doubted. 'I put it down to help with Doris.'

Rose stepped forward. She couldn't actually remember what Mrs Soames did to help Doris but she believed her when she said her handbag was gone because it was a permanent fixture on her arm and now it was nowhere to be seen.

'Somebody must have taken advantage of all the commotion and taken it,' Mrs Soames said, her mouth a thin straight line of anger.

'But who would do such a thing?' Dame Pamela cried.

'The same person who's taken the first edition?' Mrs Soames said and Rose could feel herself blushing.

'But we don't know it's been taken by anyone,' Dame Pamela said. 'It's just missing.'

'That's right,' Rose said, catching Roberta's eye. 'I'm sure the first edition will turn up.'

'Perhaps Doris Norris faked a heart attack so she could get the first edition out of here without being suspected,' Mrs Soames said.

'Oh, that's ridiculous!' Dame Pamela said but a fleeting look of doubt passed over her face as if she was weighing up the possibility.

'Everybody just calm down,' Dan said, stepping forward. 'We've all had a shock. Mrs Soames, we'll all have a good look around for your handbag.'

'I think we should call the police!' Mrs Soames said, 'and have everybody searched.'

'I'm beginning to think that's the right thing to do too,' Robyn said.

Dan turned to look at her. 'Really?'

'Well, you can't find your gold watch,' Robyn said. 'Maybe there *is* a thief amongst us.'

Warwick stepped forward and cleared his throat too. 'I've lost something as well.'

'Really?' Dame Pamela said.

'What have you lost?' Katherine asked.

'Well, it's-' he paused, 'it's a surprise.'

'But I thought you said you'd left it at home – whatever *it* is,' Katherine said, her voice laced with suspicion.

Warwick shook his head. 'The more I think about it, the more I'm convinced I packed it,' he said.

'Well, one thing's for sure – nobody's going anywhere – look,' Dan said, and everybody looked out of the hallway window as the snow began to fall thick and fast. 'We're well and truly snowed in.'

'Well, somebody's trying to get somewhere,' Roberta said as she walked over to the window.

'Oh, my god! It's that awful Jackson Moore!' Mia said as she joined Roberta.

'What's he doing going out in this weather?' Dame Pamela asked. 'I don't want any more casualties today.'

'He's running away!' Mrs Soames shouted. 'He's got my handbag – *look!*'

'Stop him!' Dame Pamela shouted.

Instantly, Dan sprang into action, opening the great front door and dashing out into the winter wonderland, his long legs sinking deep into the snow as he ran after the escapee.

'STOP!' he yelled but the man did nothing more than look behind him for a moment before stumbling on down the driveway. It was definitely Jackson Moore and Dan was furious that this man thought he had a right to come to Purley and take whatever he wanted – from his sister and from their guests.

'I said *STOP!*' Dan shouted again.

Luckily, the snow was slowing the thief down as was the enormous rucksack he had strapped to his back and it wasn't long before Dan caught up with him, grabbing the bag from behind and wrestling him to the cold ground.

'Get off me!' Jackson Moore cried, trying to get away but Dan was much too strong for him.

'You're not going anywhere,' Dan told him.

Warwick and Adam were soon by Dan's side and the three of them escorted Jackson Moore back to Purley Hall.

'Well, I never!' Dame Pamela said as the four men entered the hallway, shaking snow from their hair and their boots.

'Take the bag, Adam,' Dan said and the man was stripped of his rucksack.

'My handbag!' Mrs Soames said, stepping forward and wrenching the bag from the man's grasp before hitting him over the head with it.

'That will do, Mrs Soames,' Dan said. 'We'll let the police deal with him.'

'What are we going to do with him?' Dame Pamela asked.

'Sit him quietly in the West Drawing Room,' Dan said. 'We'll keep an eye on him. He won't go anywhere.'

Jackson Moore tried to shrug himself free of Dan but his grip was like iron.

'I expect the police will want to know exactly what he took but I'm guessing everyone wants their possessions back?' Dan said, nodding to Adam.

'I've got a camera,' Mia said, taking the world's tiniest camera out of her jacket pocket. 'I can film everything as it comes out of the bag.'

'Great idea!' Dan said.

'Oh, my goodness!' Adam said. 'It's my wallet! I didn't even know it had gone.' He reached inside the rucksack and brought out item after item.

'Who's is this ring?' Dame Pamela asked, holding up a lovely old garnet ring.

'That's Doris Norris's,' Mia said, recognising it instantly.

'Why you low down, sneaking-' Mrs Soames was at Jackson Moore again with her handbag.

'You'd better take him through to the West Drawing Room right away before Mrs Soames finishes him off,' Adam said with a wink.

Dan nodded and the traitor was led away.

Adam continued his search through the rucksack, placing items onto the side table in the hallway.

'One gold watch,' he said, handing it to Robyn.

'Thank goodness!' she said.

'A silver cross?'

'That's mine!' a young woman stepped forward to claim her missing necklace.

'And-' Adam rooted around, surfacing with a little ring box which he opened. He gave a long low whistle. 'A rather lovely antique diamond ring. Who's is this?'

A few guests moved forward to take a look but nobody claimed it.

'No sign of the first edition?' Dame Pamela asked anxiously.

'I'm afraid not,' Adam said, placing the unclaimed ring on the table and checking the side pockets of the rucksack.

'Pammy?' Dan's voice called from the West Drawing Room.

Dame Pamela walked across the hallway and disappeared into the room. Everyone waited and, a moment later, there was a cry and Dame Pamela emerged, a gigantic smile on her face.

'It's the first edition!' she said. 'He had it hidden in his jacket!'

Everybody cheered and Warwick made the most of the moment and pushed his way through the guests. 'Adam?' he said.

Adam looked up from the rucksack which he was still searching through. 'Yes? You okay? You look a bit washed out.'

'That ring box – the red one.'

Adam's eyebrows rose. 'Is that yours?'

Warwick nodded, glancing quickly behind him to check that Katherine wasn't watching.

'Ah!' Adam said with a knowing smile as he handed him the box. 'Very nice.'

Warwick quickly placed the ring box in his jacket pocket and then jumped as Katherine's arm snaked around his body.

'You were fabulous out there with Dan,' she said.

'Was I?'

'Like a hero from a Lorna Warwick novel,' she said, smiling up at him.

He grinned. 'You're so wonderful,' he told her. 'Come on. I've got a surprise for you.'

'What, right now?' Katherine said.

'Not *that* kind of surprise!' he said with a laugh. 'It's *much* better than that.'

'Really?' Katherine said. 'This I've got to see!' And the two of them left the crowd and headed up the great staircase together.

Roberta flopped down into an armchair by the bedroom window. 'I've never been so relieved in all my life!' she said.

Rose had picked up the three volumes of *Pride and Prejudice* and was flipping through the pages. 'So what edition is this, then?'

'I have absolutely no idea,' Roberta said. 'I'm only glad it's not the *first*.'

'But it looks really old. It's probably still worth tens of thousands of pounds.'

Roberta gulped and stood up. 'We have *got* to get it back to the library – right *now!*'

The two of them left the room, the three old volumes hidden in the hessian bag once more. Most of the guests had dispersed and the sisters found themselves blissfully alone in the library. They were just about to take the books out of the bag when Higgins entered.

'Can I help you, ladies?' he asked, eyeing them with suspicion.

'No, thank you,' Rose said. 'Well, actually, there *is* something you might be able to help me with but you probably don't know the answer.'

'What is it, madam?' Higgins said. 'I tend to know the answer to most questions.'

Rose nodded. 'The portrait in the hallway?'

'Of Dame Pamela? It was painted in 1977 by Robert L Sheldon.'

'No, not that one – the other one,' Rose said, skilfully leading Higgins out of the library.'

Roberta waited a moment until they were out of sight and then dived into the bag. One, two, three volumes – all neatly back on the shelf. She breathed a sigh of relief and smiled as Rose came back in.

'I hope you've done it.'

'Oh, yes,' Roberta said. 'Now, get me out of here. I don't want to see another old book as long as I live!'

CHAPTER 17

Warwick swallowed hard. The time had come. He turned to Katherine and steeled himself. He was making the right decision. He knew that. He'd never loved anyone in his life as much as Katherine and he knew he wanted to spend the rest of his life with her.

'So, what's this surprise then?' she asked crossing the room and closing the space between them.

'You know I said I'd left your Christmas present at home? Well, I didn't.'

'You found it?'

'No, Adam found it – in Jackson Moore's rucksack.'

'Jackson Moore stole my Christmas present?' Katherine said indignantly.

'But we've got it back - only the paper's gone so I'm afraid you can't unwrap it.' He cleared his throat. 'Merry Christmas, Katherine.'

As soon as Katherine saw the tiny box, she gasped. There was only one thing a box like this could hold and that was a ring. She looked up at Warwick.

'Open it,' he said.

Her fingers shook as she opened the box. It was a beautiful diamond ring – its single stone almost smoky with age.

'Do you like it?' Warwick dared to ask.

'Warwick – I *love* it.'

'Because I can get you a modern ring if you prefer. Only I found this amazing place which specialises in antique jewellery and this is Georgian. Well, the guy said it was Georgian. Maybe it's just old, I don't know.'

'No, it's Georgian,' Katherine said. 'Warwick, is this what I think it is?'

He smiled hesitantly at her. 'I'm not going to tell a lady which finger to wear a ring on but I'm hoping – very much – that you'll wear it on this one.' He picked up her left hand and kissed her ring finger.

'Oh, Warwick!'

'Katherine, will you marry me?'

Katherine's eyes glittered with tears. 'Yes,' she whispered. 'I'll marry you.'

They kissed and then they hugged and then they cried and then Warwick placed the ring on Katherine's finger, his hands shaking with excitement.

'It's so beautiful,' Katherine said.

'No, *you're* so beautiful,' Warwick told her, 'and I love you so much.'

'I love you too,' Katherine said and they kissed again.

'Are you all right?' Warwick asked a moment later.

'I'm fine,' Katherine said, blinking her tears away.

'Are you sure?' He stroked her hair and gazed at her. 'You look,' he paused, 'a bit dazed!'

Katherine laughed. 'I am,' she said. 'I never thought that you were planning this. I thought-'

'What?' Warwick said, his head cocked to one side.

'I thought you were up to something.'

'What do you mean?'

'I don't know,' she said, 'but you were making me anxious and I didn't know what to think.'

'Katherine!' he cried. 'You know I wouldn't hide anything from you – nothing terrible, anyway! You *must* know that by now.'

She nodded. 'I'm so sorry,' she said, trying to banish the insecurities of her past.

'But I had to hide this from you because it was a surprise!' he said.

'I know!' Katherine said.

'And it was a good surprise, wasn't it?' he asked, a tiny smile on his face.

'It was the best surprise in the world,' she said.

'Good,' he said and they kissed again.

'Hey,' Katherine said a moment later, a huge smile on her face, 'maybe Dame Pamela will let us get married here!'

Warwick laughed. 'A wedding at Purley?' he said. 'What a *wonderful* idea!'

Jackson Moore hadn't said a single thing since being shoved unceremoniously into the West Drawing Room an hour ago. Dan and Adam were standing guard, watching as their prisoner sat hunched in the corner of the room, muttering incomprehensibly to himself and occasionally stroking his moustache. Higgins had brought in tea and scones but he hadn't touched anything.

Dan looked at his recently-found watch. 'Well, the police should be here at any moment.'

'They said they were coming by road?' Adam said.

'Apparently, the roads aren't as bad as we think outside Church Stinton but this last stretch is pretty hairy and we might have to walk him down the driveway.'

Adam nodded. 'I used to want to be a policeman when I was about four.'

'Me too,' Dan said and they grinned at each other. 'Listen, I'm going to ring the hospital again to check on Doris. Will you be all right keeping an eye on our fugitive for a moment?'

'Sure thing,' Adam said. 'If he tries to steal those scones, I'll call through for assistance.'

Dan saluted him and left the room.

Dame Pamela, Robyn, Cassie and Benedict were sitting in the library by the fire when Dan entered.

'I've finally been able to talk to someone at the hospital,' he said. 'Doris is going to be fine. She *did* have a heart attack but she's stable now and her family has been contacted.'

'Oh, thank goodness!' Dame Pamela said.

'Poor Doris! This is one Christmas she'll never forget,' Robyn said, kissing the top of Cassie's head as Dan joined them by the fire.

VICTORIA CONNELLY

'It's a Christmas *none* of us are going to forget,' Dan said. 'And there's news from the police too,' he added. 'Apparently, Jackson Moore's got previous charges against him. It seems he goes from conference to conference preying on unsuspecting victims.'

'So, he wasn't a Janeite after all,' Robyn said. 'I was talking to Mia and Kay and we were all suspicious about him.'

Dame Pamela shook her head. 'I still can't believe he thought he'd get away with it. It was badly done, wasn't it, Higgins?' she said as her butler entered the room.

'It certainly was, madam.'

'Yes, he shouldn't have picked on Jane Austen fans,' Robyn said. 'He met his match this time.'

Dame Pamela smiled. 'He most certainly did.' Her gaze settled on Benedict and she let out a long sigh. 'And I owe somebody an apology,' she said. 'I'm so sorry I suspected you, Benedict.'

'All in the past, Pamsy,' he said with a smile.

'I was just so confused by everything and, well, you must admit that we don't see you very often.'

He nodded. 'I know and that's something I was trying to make amends for.'

'Really? That's why you're here?'

Benedict gave a funny little cough. 'Well, I – erm – I had a bit of a scare recently.'

'What sort of a scare?' Dan asked.

'A medical scare,' Benedict said.

'Oh, god! Are you all right?' Dan said.

'I'm absolutely fine,' Benedict said. 'Had a spot of cancer but it's all fine now,' he said, casually waving a hand, as if it might have been a common cold he'd caught. 'Only these things make a chap think, don't you know, and I realised I wasn't spending enough time with the people I love most in the world.'

'Oh, Benedict! You know you're always welcome here, don't you?' Dame Pamela crossed the room and Benedict stood up to receive her hug. 'You should have told us!'

'I don't like to worry anybody,' he said.

'But that's a big sister's job – to worry about her little brother.'

Dan stood up and gave Benedict a hug too. 'You're sure you're okay?'

'Never better, Danny boy. Never better.'

Dan took a deep breath. 'Good heavens! What a day. How's about a drink, everyone?'

'How's about some mulled wine?' Dame Pamela said.

Higgins went off to fetch the mulled wine, bringing back a large silver jug and four thick glass goblets.

'This is certainly one conference that shall go down in the history of Purley Hall,' Dame Pamela said as she gave her ruby earrings a little tug and thanked her lucky stars that none of her jewels had seen the inside of Jackson Moore's pockets.

'I hope it hasn't put you off running them,' Robyn said, worried in case Dame Pamela was leading up to saying just that.

Dame Pamela finished her mulled wine and held her glass out to Higgins for a refill. 'Of course it hasn't, my dear. Jane Austen fans are made of strong stuff. In fact, I was just thinking of an Easter conference. What do you think? Perhaps we can discuss it after a little bite to eat. Higgins? I think mince pies are in order, don't you?'

'Certainly, madam,' Higgins said and he left the room forthwith.

***

ABOUT THE AUTHOR

Victoria Connelly was brought up in Norfolk and studied English literature at Worcester University before becoming a teacher in North Yorkshire. After getting married in a medieval castle in the Yorkshire Dales and living in London for eleven years, she moved to rural Suffolk where she lives with her artist husband and a mad Springer spaniel and ex-battery hens.

Her first novel, Flights of Angels, was published in Germany and made into a film. Victoria and her husband flew out to Berlin to see it being filmed and got to be extras in it.

Five of her novels have been Kindle bestsellers.

If you'd like to contact Victoria or sign up for her newsletter about future releases, visit her website www.victoriaconnelly.com.

She's also on Facebook and Twitter @VictoriaDarcy

ALSO BY VICTORIA CONNELLY

Austen Addicts Series
A Weekend with Mr Darcy
The Perfect Hero
published in the US as Dreaming of Mr Darcy
Mr Darcy Forever
Happy Birthday, Mr Darcy

Other Fiction
Molly's Millions
The Runaway Actress
Wish You Were Here
Flights of Angels
Unmasking Elena Montella
Three Graces
It's Magic (A compilation volume: Flights of Angels,
Unmasking Elena Montella and Three Graces)

Short Story Collections
One Perfect Week and other stories
The Retreat and other stories
Postcard from Venice and other stories

Non-fiction
Escape to Mulberry Cottage

Children's Adventure
Secret Pyramid

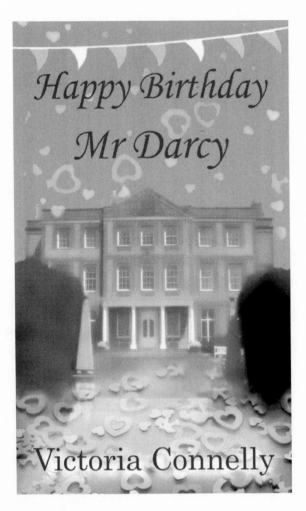

Happy Birthday Mr Darcy

Victoria Connelly

The next exciting story – out now.

8754134R10073

Made in the USA
San Bernardino, CA
21 February 2014